A Girl Called Ari

By P. J. Sky

A Girl Called Ari is a work of fiction. Names, characters,
places, events and incidents are the products of the
author's imagination or are used fictitiously.

First edition

Cover artwork by AutumnSky.co.uk

For Katherine

THE ADVENTURES OF ARI

#1

A GIRL CALLED ARI

CHAPTER 1

Later, once she'd returned to the walled city, with its cold comforts of air conditioning and an endless supply of syntho, Starla Corinth found herself increasingly drawn back to the surrounding wasteland, and the pale-eyed girl she knew as Ari. The events that lead to the intersection of their lives, for under ordinary circumstances they never would have met, were never entirely resolved, but for Starla they appeared to begin the night of her 18th birthday. She'd been late for a party she'd no wish to attend, and in the descending elevator, she'd fidgeted with the straps of her dress. With his latest adjustments, it was almost as if the couturier intended her to suffocate. The blue velvet hugged her slender frame, but most striking were her deep blue eyes which shone like storm-flecked sapphires.

The elevator slowed and came to rest on the ninety-second floor. On the other side of the mirrored doors, Starla heard the hubbub of a party already underway. She inspected her eyeshadow, and in the golden light, her long eyelashes sparkled.

Starla, she told herself, you look perfect.

She'd lied; her nose was too angular, her jaw too like her father's.

She wasn't sure when she'd first started talking to herself, but now it came naturally, she'd spent so long alone.

As the elevator doors slid open, the applause struck Starla like an aerial assault. On a platform, raised high above the crowds, waited her father; a red tuxedo, a mop of silver hair, a hooked nose that looked like it had once been broken but left slightly deformed. His smile was warm, easy, and impossible to read. Like the city perimeter, his face was a wall. As mayor of the city, Titus Corinth stood at the centre of his world, above his subjects, in a hall full of bright lights and polished chromium.

As she stepped from the elevator, someone clutched her arm. Alarmed, she tried to pull away. The grip tightened. Starla's heart quickened. She looked at the young man in the light blue uniform, someone from the praetorian guard. Sandy blonde hair and wide, brown eyes. The eyes looked scared. There was something familiar about him, she'd seen him somewhere before. He'd been watching her from afar. He leant in and spoke, his voice almost a whisper.

"Miss Corinth, you're in danger."

Starla wrenched her arm free and fell backwards into the throng. Hands caught her. The applause had stopped, replaced by calls and shouts. More guards appeared, pushing the crowds back, clearing a path to the stage. Shaken, Starla straightened her dress and scanned the faces in the crowd. Sandy blonde hair and wide, brown eyes. The face was gone. Now, there were too many uniforms, and too many confused faces.

"Please please," said her father from the stage. "There has been some confusion. Let my daughter through."

Starla looked up to her father who still stood on the platform, his hand reached out to her. He hadn't moved. In his face, could she recognise any form of concern? If he had any, he didn't show it. And now more than ever, Starla wanted to leave the party. She remembered the words.

Danger.

She looked again at the faces around her. They were waiting for her to react. But how could she react? How should she react? The other guards, ever-present in their light blue uniforms, stood motionless between her and the crowd. But they didn't look at the crowd, they looked at her.

Catching her breath, her heart still racing, Starla approached the stage. Behind her, the crowds filled her path like a closing jaw.

Her father's smile widened. "So, without further delay, let me present the first daughter of our blessed community."

Mounting the steps, she took his hand. This physical contact with her father was rare. His hand was large, cold and oddly angular, and a shiver ran down her spine. She remembered the hand clasping her arm.

Danger.

Her father leant forward. "I'm sorry my dear, I'm not sure what that was about."

Her father returned his attention to the audience. "We must thank you all for gracing us with your presence on this most special of days. My friends, it does us both great honour to have you here tonight."

Starla's heart still galloped and she fought the urge to pull her hand free.

"Today is important," her father continued. "Today we come together and celebrate. However... my daughter's birthday is not all we celebrate. For at these times we also celebrate ourselves and our city. This humble beacon of civilisation. This place of hope, of purpose, of community and of citizenship."

As her father continued this familiar speech, Starla thought again of the face of the guard. She thought of the soft, grey rings beneath his eyes.

"Here, we each form part of something much greater than ourselves. And we make a choice, to live in this place, and to live by our rules, our laws, and to practice our way of life." Her father paused. When he continued, his voice was lower. "No one more than I understands just how precious and delicate that is. Leadership is a heavy burden, and one I do not take lightly."

Briefly, he glanced at Starla, and when she caught his eye she shuddered. It was dark and calculated and, just for a moment, she felt like prey.

Again, she remembered those wide, brown eyes.

His voice fell lower still. "I would do absolutely anything to protect this city and our way of life."

His words were followed by a hot, airless silence.

Danger.

A tray floated above the audience, upon which stood two flutes of synthesised blue champagne. Against the thin stem, Starla's fingers trembled.

I just want this to be over, she thought. I want to be away from these people and these lights and from my father. I want to be far away from here.

The mayor raised his glass. "And so I propose a toast, to my beautiful daughter Starla, and, to the city."

△△△

The balcony that overlooked the city was quiet and almost deserted, the sounds of the city muted in the great bowl of the starry sky. The glowing buildings stretched out all around, jagged sky-scrapers caught in a web of neon monorail. Far below, Bath and Parsons Street thronged with people, vehicles, and yellow light. But, beyond the luminous structures, the world fell abruptly into darkness. Occasionally, beyond the wall, flickers of orange moved in the inky blackness.

Starla took a gulp of the blue champagne. The sweet liquid burnt the back of her throat. She remembered the words of the young guardsman. It had happened so quickly. Now, it was almost as if it hadn't happened at all. At the edge of the balcony, she leant over the railing. The wind stung her face and she turned her head against it. She let the cool air fill her lungs and the tremble in her hands slowed.

Danger.

It was probably nothing. Who can touch me here? But what had my father meant back there...

Looking upwards, her eyes caught the glint of Velle Stella.

Do I take Velle Stella's name, or does it take mine?

As a thousand disparate pinpricks moved slowly across the dark sky, just one remained tethered. Faintly blue, the star that never moved.

Velle. To wish.

I wish I could escape this place. I wish I could be normal, and live a normal life. That's the real danger, to spend my whole life in this tower, wondering about such remote things as stars, while everyone around me either grovels at my feet or wants to stab me in the back. If I'm in danger, I'd rather confront it head on, instead of this slow death at the top of this tower.

She let her eyes fall to the darkness.

What lies beyond the wall?

She'd often asked this question, it had a certain self-destructive thrill. The ultimate escape. Public information films told of a barbarous land populated by cannibalistic mutants hell bent on the destruction of themselves and the city. A noxious wasteland that stretched as far as the eye could see. Therefore, there was the wall, a protective rampart between civilisation and the savage. Only here in the city was anyone truly safe.

Starla imagined lush forests, rolling fields and snow-capped mountains, like the ancient landscape paintings in the city archives, peeking out from behind the portraits of long dead kings and queens. Many of these paintings included walled cities like her own. However, these images didn't fit the harsh, toxic reality portrayed in the films. Poison, disease, if you were lucky and not first found by the mutants. For good reason, no one could enter the city from the outside, and those who chose to leave could never return. The ultimate penalty and punishment was exile.

Her father leant against the railing. "You know my dear, for a moment I had wondered if you were going to join us."

Starla stiffened. "I wasn't going to miss it,

was I?" She glanced sideways at her father. "How could I?"

The mayor smiled, but the smile only reinforced their mutual divide. So often, he was politician rather than father.

"My dear, you know you mean much more to me than you think. And don't think I don't notice your little attempts to provoke me. But, I think you'll find you and I are far more alike than you think."

Starla looked back at the luminous buildings. "I have to say, I don't see it."

But she did. He was distant, difficult, and cold, yet each day she wondered if she was becoming more like him. She would sit at her dressing table, studying her features, searching for likeness. She had her father's forthright cheekbones, her father's triangular jaw. She wondered from whom she'd gained her eyes. She'd never known her mother.

I am my father's daughter, and he leads this city. He commands power. Perhaps, with every passing day, I'm becoming more like him. Perhaps this is my fate.

Danger.

For a moment, Starla's heartbeat quickened.

"Well, you will my dear, in time... Tell me, have you given any more thought to our little discussion?"

Starla's grip on the rail tightened.

"No," she said. "I haven't."

"Well my dear, keep it in mind. You must understand, all this is so much bigger than you or I. Sometimes, you must place your own feelings aside for a greater purpose."

"And what purpose is that?"

"The city, of course. The transition of power…"

"Well, I've not thought about it."

She glanced at her father and, just briefly, she glimpsed something in his eyes. It was almost as if he was scared. His request gave her power. It was only a moment, and then it was gone. The wind caught her hair and she turned away and shuddered.

Her father continued. "We must secure a lasting future for the city."

"It's my choice, Father."

Her father sighed. "Well, if you won't think about it…" He trailed off and they both stood in silence.

If I accept this, thought Starla, I'll never be free. But he can't force me, not this time. Yet, at the back of her mind, doubt niggled. Can he make me do this? So little of my life is mine to choose.

A tall young man approached.

"Ahh," said her father, "Master Panache."

Starla rolled her eyes. Of course it was.

"Well my dear, I will leave you in the capable hands of Mr. Panache." He gave her shoulder a gentle squeeze and Starla stiffened. Quietly he added, "Try to enjoy your evening. And please, think about what I've said."

He left them and Max sidled alongside.

"Hell of a speech."

Starla sighed. "You reckon?"

Max leant across the railing and spat over the side of the building. He righted himself and gave Starla a sideways grin. Starla had known Max all her life. A little older and slightly taller, he was the closest thing she had to a brother. He was the son of Agrippa Panache, her father's closest ally, and biggest rival. His father's position as praetor made Agrippa Panache the second most important person in the city.

Max said, "I liked the dancing."

Starla raised her eyebrow. "The dancing?"

"Sure, when I woke this morning, I didn't expect to see our city's leader shake his hips like that." Max rolled his hips in a little dance.

The right corner of Starla's lip curled slightly upwards.

"Ahh, she smiled." Max grinned. "I saw that Starla. You can't take that back."

Starla caught herself and straightened her lip.

Max was handsome in a way, with a solid, round jawbone and two prominent cheekbones. Along with his fresh, pale skin, illuminated now in the multi-coloured lights, his face managed to look both sturdy and fragile, as if he'd evolved to match the many spindle-like structures of the city. Above his large, flat forehead was a head of wavy blonde hair, always slightly unkempt.

Max leant forward and lowered his voice. "Look, I'm sorry about earlier. You know, I know what your father wants. He wants the same thing mine does. But, all this stuff about marriage, it's not for me. So to hell with what our parents say."

"Really?"

"Really," said Max. He leant out across the city and cried; "To hell with you all." He turned back, still grinning. "They don't get to decide how we live our lives. They're not the future."

"And tell me, what is?"

"We are, Starla, you and I. And we can do with it what we want."

"I should warn you Max, you're in danger of sounding like a politician."

Max shrugged. "I hope not. I don't want to end up sounding like my father. Fact is our parents don't really care about us. We're just pawns in their game. All they care about is the city, and now they're scared."

For a moment, Max's thoughts sounded frighteningly like Starla's own.

"Scared?"

Max nodded. "They're scared because they know this city won't be theirs forever. Times will change, and they won't be able to control it. But, enough about the city…" He pushed forward his glass and let it touch Starla's. In the city lights, his green eyes sparkled. "You only turn eighteen once. So happy birthday. And to many more, hopefully not quite like this one."

Starla sipped and eyed Max suspiciously. He averted her gaze and looked back across the city. His busy fingers toyed with the stem of his wine glass.

A tray floated towards them containing a carefully constructed tower of syntho cubes in purple and blue, each one a perfect mouthful of synthesised goodness. Out of habit, Starla took one, though she wasn't hungry.

Whatever he says, thought Starla, he's playing a game. I know Max too well. But whatever his game is, I won't be the prize.

She bit into the delicately sweet syntho cube. She barely had to chew it.

Max reached up and undid the top button of his shirt. He caught Starla's eye again and grinned. "Good?"

Starla nodded.

"Ahh, I prefer the mauve."

Starla swallowed and felt slightly dizzy again.

The balcony doors opened and Liviana Panache, Max's sister, glided through them. She gave Starla a tight-lipped smile and, in return, Starla considered how Liviana would look tripping over her voluminous pink ball gown. So heavily made up, below a shock of luminous pink hair, Liviana's face looked like it had been cast from plastic. Chin thrust forward, eyes narrowed, her white lips formed a small, impish right angle.

"Starla, my dear."

"Liviana," Starla replied. "I'm so glad that you could join us."

Liviana pushed alongside Starla and nudged her with her elbow. "Seeing you in that dress again, you know I think it does work after all."

Inwardly, Starla cringed, and fought the urge to push Liviana over the balcony railing. "Well, Liviana, I'll take that as a compliment." Starla felt certain this close proximity was deliberate, as if Liviana knew it made her uncomfortable.

"That's what I love about you Starla, you're so like your father. If you take to something, you stick right with it, no matter what anyone else thinks."

"And who cares what anyone else thinks?" said Max. He winked at Starla. "Starla, tonight you look lovely."

Starla rolled her eyes. Liviana was harmless enough. She wished she'd just go away and leave her alone on the balcony.

Alone with Max though? The thought caught her off-guard.

Liviana's eyes widened. "Brother dear, I didn't say she didn't look lovely."

"Well," said Starla. "Let me be the first to congratulate you on your choice of dress this evening."

Liviana grinned. "Starla dear, you're just too kind."

"I really am."

Liviana's smile faltered and her eyes narrowed. Liviana raised her glass, as if to propose a toast, and then tipped its contents down the front of Starla's dress.

"Oh Starla, I'm sorry."

Starla glared at Liviana and her hands began to tremble.

"I didn't mean it," said Liviana, a grin forming.

"What do you mean, you..."

"I didn't."

But Starla had only to look into Liviana's eyes to know the real story.

Well, what are you going to do about it Starla?

And Starla wanted to strike Liviana. She wanted to wipe that nasty smirk from her sickeningly angelic face. Enough was enough, the accumulated aggression of years of putdowns and slights. The tendons of her right hand quivered, only Liviana wasn't worth it. It was the scene Liviana wanted, right here, with all of city society watching.

"Honestly," said Liviana. "It was just an accident." She didn't even have the decency not to smile.

Starla placed her glass on the ledge below the railing. "Whatever." She turned her back on the Panache siblings. Max managed, "But Starla...," before she was through the double doors.

How could Liviana do that? Here, and in front of everyone on tonight of all nights. I hate them. I hate the whole Panache family. I don't care if they own the whole damn city.

In the bathroom, the stalls were empty. Starla leant against the blue marble countertop and stared at her reflection and her dress melted into the deep blue walls. She didn't care about the dress, but her eyes were moist, and the blue makeup had started to smudge.

I hate her.

I must rise above her though. Liviana is no one, that's why she has to slight me, it's all she has, but I'm first daughter of the city. Appearance is everything.

Her father had told her this. You can't lead the city without looking like a leader. And, if you look like a leader, and you act like a leader, you are a leader.

She drew deep breaths and inspected her blue eyeshadow.

Liviana's a bitch. She'll get hers one day.

A short while later, the elevator hummed quietly as it worked its way to the roof. Far below, the sounds of the party receded. Starla closed her eyes and slowly exhaled. Did she even want to go back to the party? Her part was done, and Liviana didn't matter, none of them mattered.

I'm a Corinth, she thought, and above their stupid games. I refuse to play them. They can do what they like, I won't rise to it.

The elevator came to rest and, with sigh, the mirrored doors slid open.

To hell with you all.

She remembered Max's words and caught herself smiling.

What is wrong with me? Smiling at something Max said.

She'd almost forgotten the spilled champagne.

Stepping into the corridor, a cloth pressed over Starla's nose and mouth. It smelt faintly sweet and her head began to spin. Someone was behind her. A cold shiver ran down her spine as she realised what was happening, then darkness folded around her.

CHAPTER 2

That afternoon, Starla had sat alone at her marble-topped dressing table, chin resting in her palm, and watched the single ornamental fish swim in circles in the bowl by her makeup box. The fat blue and white fish twitched and waved its fins aimlessly, gulping at the clear liquid. It stared back with bulbous black eyes.

I should run away, she thought. I could disappear, show them I'm no pawn.

She dipped her delicate forefinger into the water. The fish rose up, hovered just below her fingertip, and swam back down.

They wouldn't miss me, not after the speech. Two minutes on stage, that's all my father needs. Why is tonight so important to him?

Well, they can wait. After all, I'm the mayor's daughter. Stuck high in this glass tower, I spend my whole life waiting…

△△△

Starla lurched awake.

Where am I?

Beneath, the greasy floor she lay on vibrated with a low rumble. She felt a forward motion. The floor jolted. Starla's heart started to race.

She kicked out, struck the wall, and a sharp pain burst through her toes. She inhaled sharply. With blurry eyes, she squinted at her surroundings. Above, through thin windows, yellow sunlight spilled onto the floor and the metal wall opposite. Her left shoulder and hip throbbed. At the back of her head, a dull pain had started to form. Her shoulders were pulled backwards, hands held together at the base of her spine. When she tried to move them, the cord pinched her wrists.

Starla's chest tightened, she broke into a cold sweat.

Something's wrong, she thought.

The interior swayed.

I must escape.

Contorting her legs, Starla slid herself up against the wall. She sat and, with legs like jelly, she used the wall to push herself to her feet. Like the floor, the metal wall vibrated. Using it to steady herself, she craned her head to the thin windows.

Beyond the cracked glass, a sea of red dust ran

all the way to the horizon, vast and flat and sweeping by along the side of the road.

Starla's heart skipped. She was on the outside.

Her mind filled with the images of mutants, their skin melted, and the yellow warning signs with black skulls above crossed femurs.

Starla staggered from the window.

I can't be on the outside.

She stumbled to the small window set in the double doors at the rear. Split and blistered, a dilapidated tarmac road flowed out in a cloud of red dust.

She took in sharp, shallow breaths. Her heart thumped against the walls of her chest.

This can't be happening. This must be some mistake. I can't be here, not on the outside.

Headache, fatigue, nausea, vomiting, red blisters. Starla recalled the laundry list of symptoms, drummed into her, in the event she should find herself outside the wall. She shuddered and bile rose in her throat.

Swaying, Starla tugged against her binds. Her eyes began to tear. Outside, she passed by a cart pulled by donkeys, heavily laden with some kind of dirty looking rubble. The scrawny animals strained against their ropes, ribs visible under a threadbare fleece, a grey tongue lolling from a gaping mouth. At the edge of the road, wrapped in shabby cloaks, anonymous figures crouched, their faces hidden, bony hands clasping rusty implements. Starla imagined their disfigured faces, their features melted beyond all recognition of anything once human. Eyes misaligned, noses without angles, mouths unable to form the basic patterns of speech. Starla's head began to swim.

I must get back to the city.

The vehicle thudded and Starla lost her footing. She hit the floor and pain ruptured along her pelvis. Gasping, she tugged again at her binds. Where they pinched, her skin now burned. She tasted salty tears. At the back of her throat, a round lump began to form.

Stupid girl, you have to figure this out.

With deep breaths, she willed herself to calm.

She pushed herself back into the corner. Carefully, she explored her binds. Poking her index fingers towards each other, she felt either side of a round knot. She began to work her fingers against the knot. When the vehicle thudded again, she lost her place.

Come on Starla, you have to do this.

She began again, working her fingers from either side. The vehicle bounced, slamming her against the wall.

"Dag it!"

It was no use.

She was on her side again, back at the start. Sweat poured from ever part of her body. From beneath, the floor vibrations rolled through her skull.

What do they want from me? Do these people not know who my father is? They won't get away with this. I'm certain to be rescued soon.

Above, beyond the glass, the sky was pale blue. Tears blurred her vision and she shut her eyes. The metal box felt smaller, as if the panels were moving in.

How long have I been in this box, outside the wall? How long since exposure… Am I yet even exposed, or in here am I somehow protected? But, she assured herself, I'll be rescued soon.

Juddering, the vehicle began to slow. Again, Starla's heart began to race.

Starla got to her feet and peered out of the windows. At first, there was the only the flat red dust. The vehicle rumbled passed a line of camels, all strung together, heavily laden with bulky sacks. The animals looked back indifferently, rolling their angular jaws. Through the rear window, the train disappeared into the dust.

Then the vehicle slowed to a halt.

Close by the road sat a corral full of animals; camels, donkeys and sheep. There were huge mounds of red rubble and carts laden with fat sacks. Starla saw three men approach the vehicle, shabby and gaunt, their skin a leathery patchwork of dark blotches and deep creases. But they didn't have the melted deformities of the mutants.

Could these men have some connection with the city?

Heavily bearded, the eldest of the three wore

a big grin. He looked like he might have recently shared a joke with the other two, but they didn't appear amused. He walked with an easy gait, his shoulders loose and his stride amiable. The other two looked younger, though their skin still seemed prematurely aged. They hung back, their eyes wide and their movements jittery. Just below the shoulder, each wore a bright red armband. And in their hands, each cradled a large gun.

Perhaps, wondered Starla, I should attract their attention.

On tiptoes, Starla pressed her nose against the glass. Despite a lack of obvious deformities, the men looked utterly alien.

The older man raised his gun and fired into the front of the vehicle.

Starla's heart leapt.

The muffled popping reverberated through the metal panels.

The vehicle lurched forwards and Starla fell backwards. Then the vehicle stopped again. More gunshots followed, and then muffled yells and the sound of breaking glass.

Starla pushed herself towards the back of the vehicle. The world fell silent, the floor no longer vibrated. The engine had stopped. Then, passing on the other side of the metal panel, Starla heard footsteps. A cold shiver ran down her spine.

Starla, you have to do something. You have to protect yourself.

Her damp dress stuck to her skin. She struggled again against the binds.

The doors flexed. Someone was trying them from the other side.

Starla, if they come in here they will do something terrible to you. You, Starla Corinth, the mayor's daughter, first daughter of the city. You're eighteen now, you have to do better than this Starla. You have to.

She leant against the doors and pushed herself to her feet, avoiding the rear window. She positioned herself between the double doors.

Starla, this is insane. Whatever you're doing, this isn't a plan.

Behind the doors, she heard the tin cry of bending metal. Then the doors were wrenched open and Starla fell forward.

The harsh white light blinded her. She struck something soft and moving. Arms, neck, fabric. A head, a chest.

"Wahhhh"

A man was beneath her, flat on his back.

The heat, the dust.

Starla looked up, squinting. She saw one of the younger men approach, his gun raised.

Come on Starla, get up.

She pushed her knee against the chest of the man beneath her. It felt fragile, like it might give way. Rising, she ploughed into the other man and knocked him off his feet. She tried to kick him but her tight dress stopped her.

She stumbled. Something struck the side of

her head hard. She barely felt it. It struck her again. She turned towards it and found herself starring down the barrel of a gun.

△△△

"Hey there missy, you just calm down now or else we're gonna 'ave to shoot ya."

The older man examined her from down the barrel of the gun. Starla felt something wet trickle down her skull. She held her breath. Her heart thumped.

Were they infected?

The younger man, whom Starla had just knocked over, was getting up. The wrist and elbow joints of his bare arms were like knots in a frayed rope. Gaunt hollows formed in his cheeks. One bloodshot eye darted between her and his companions, the other milky white.

The third man still lay flat on his back. "Boss," he said. "I can't feel my legs."

"Shut up ya drongo," the older man replied. "Now then, what's a sheila like you doin' locked up in the back of that van? What makes ya so bloody valuable?"

He doesn't know who I am, thought Starla. He's no idea.

"Look at ya. Fancy clothes, fancy hair. If I didn't know better, I'd say you were from the big smoke. Is that it? From the city?"

"Maybe."

The older man's grin widened. "So that's it. Reprobate from the big smoke. Exile from Alice. Found yourself in the wider world did ya? Well, just think of us as your personal welcomin' committee."

"Boss, please," pleaded the man lying on his back. "I can't feel my legs. I can't feel nothin'."

"You okay Spud?" asked the man with the milky eye, his gun lowered.

"He's fine. We're all fine. Just takin' in the afternoon air. Ain't that right missy? See, way I see it, you an' I could just get back in that van and we could all have ourselves a little party. A sort 'a welcome to Cooper eh?"

Starla shuddered. Her eyes darted between her assailants. The older man grinned sickeningly and licked his lips. She couldn't see the man on the ground, but the man with the milky eye looked seriously at the older man.

"He said she was worth somethin'."

"Didn't say what she was though did he," said the older man. "Just said somethin' of value. Far as I know, she ain't even 'ere. We could strike a deal missy. I reckon a sheila like you'd see a deal for the value it is out 'ere. See, city folk like you don't know how it is 'ere. Ya get yourselves into trouble real quick. An' you don't wanna go where we're supposed to take ya. I can tell ya that for free. You could see this as ya second chance, eh?"

"This ain't right," said the man with the

31

milky eye. "He said she was worth somethin'."

"Ya got a lot to learn sprog, an' I say you should watch an' learn. You'll be right won't ya missy?"

Starla shivered. She nodded nervously, her pulse beating in her ears. From somewhere over in the corral, a sheep bleated. Starla realised how quiet it was out here.

"Easy now, back in the van then." The older man began lowering his gun and inching forward.

Starla stepped backwards, towards the open doors of the van. She looked at the man with the milky eye and he looked back pitifully, his one eye wide. He was shaking too. She leant against the doorsill.

"I can't get back up," she said. "You'll need to untie me."

"Now, that hardly seems necessary." The older man placed his gun on the floor of the van. His hands started to shake; his face was slick with sweat. "See, I'm always ready to help a sheila, 'specially one bein' so obligin' of an older fella." He was close to her now and she could smell his sour stench, his breath acidic and rotten. He winked at her and Starla's stomach began to turn.

She glanced at the man with the milky eye. Please, she prayed, do something.

The man with the milky eye raised his gun and pressed the end of the barrel to the older man's left temple. "She's worth somethin'. That's what he said an' ya don't cross 'im. I know that, you know that. No one ever crosses 'im so don't lose ya head to no sheila."

The older man's eyes widened and his grin changed from menace to guilt.

"Now then son, don't get like that." He raised his sweaty hands and looked at the younger man. "I was just obligin' the lady. No one's goin' against the big fella. So why don't ya just put the gun down eh, an' we can all rest easy."

"She comes with us."

"Of course son, of course. Maybe it was my mistake. Can't blame an old man for tryin' now can ya, eh?"

For a long moment, the two men locked eyes.

"Easy now son, don't do nothin' stupid now."

Starla could see the younger man's finger shivering on the trigger. She tensed, holding her breath. With his one good eye, the younger man blinked.

The older man lunged for his gun. Starla raised her knee and aimed her kick at the older man's crotch. She slipped on the doorframe, briefly lost balance, and hit the younger man in the leg. His gun went off.

Deafened.

The older man's body fell forwards onto the floor of the van. Red blood splattered across the metal interior. The man with the milky eye let out a yelp of surprise. Starla got to her feet and started to run. She heard one of the men crying, "What 'ave ya done?"

Any moment, she thought, they'll start shooting. They'll aim their guns and bring me down.

She ran on, away from the road. She passed by the corral and sprinted into the desert. She stumbled over rocks and dirt, trying to maintain her balance with her hands bound behind her back. Her eyes blurred with tears. She scrambled down a hill and the road and corral slipped silently away. The hot air burnt her throat. Her feet slipped on the loose ground and she slowed.

Then she tripped and rolled down the hill.

She fell down a hole, banged her head, and everything went dark again.

CHAPTER 3

Ari Quinn spent her days digging salt from the bed of a long dead sea. Under the baking sun, she toiled on the salt flats, filling two rusty buckets with the dirty brown rock salt she dug up with her bare hands. Once full, she affixed them to a metal yoke and carried them over her shoulders, up the bank to where the quartermaster sat in his wheelchair in his little tent in the shade. She placed each bucket on his scales, and duly he added a mark by her name. Then she added their contents to the great mounds of salt that would, in due course, be packed onto camels and sent to the city. Then Ari took her buckets and yoke and went back down to the salt flats and did it all again. She did this every day. It was hard but steady work, and it let her keep to herself. It was better than searching for opals in the old mine shafts which was dangerous. Or, relocating to the ore mines and whatever fate that held. She'd never known anyone to return from the ore mines; either it was far better than here, or else it was far worse. And it was certainly better than the coal mines. At this memory, Ari shuddered, shutting out the months in those long, dark tunnels. It was a memory she never wanted to return to.

It was especially hot that day and Ari's throat was parched. The tang of salt and red dust hung on her lips. Briefly, she stopped filling the buckets. She got out her canteen and took a few swallows of the metallic tasting water. She coughed a little and with her palm, she wiped beads of sweat from her shaven head, feeling the tiny bristles. A welcome breeze slipped across the plain, but otherwise there was no shelter here.

In the haze, not too far away, a scrawny Angu woman, her dark skin baked hard to a leathery shell, was working the ground with a pickaxe. Bent over, her back hunched, the woman used the tool to lever up wedges of the salty crust.

Maybe, wondered Ari, I should get a pickaxe.

Pickaxes were hard to come by though, she'd have to use a lot of half-moon coins.

Would it really be easier? How long would it take to earn the coins back?

She looked at her own dry and calloused hands, powdered white with the salt. To buy a pickaxe would be making a plan. It would be committing to this place forever. That's what's wrong with buying a pickaxe. First you buy a pickaxe, then you buy a shovel, then you're wheeling a cart down here. It's become a plan. But, there is no future here. Here is existing.

You could go to the ore mines, she thought.

But no, that's worse. Then you're signing up to slave drivers. This was hard yak all right, but that was worse. Better to die here, digging up salt with your bare hands, than go there. At least here you're free. But free to do what? To go back to the city? It was impossible. Outsiders weren't allowed, and that was what she was now.

Then why not give in and go to the mines? Better yet, why not buy a pickaxe?

She looked at the Angu woman again.

If I don't leave this place, that's me in ten years. Just as much a slave as I would be in the mines. So you have to make some plan Ari, or you're gonna die here. You're gonna die in a place you were never even supposed to be.

But that's all in the past, she told herself. Ain't no sense thinking like that now.

But this place'll kill you Ari. You think that woman's gonna last many more seasons? She can't stand straight now. I bet the ore mines wouldn't even take her, and nor would anyone else.

Sighing, she got back on her knees and continued to shovel salt into her buckets.

Later, with the big red sun eating into the horizon, Ari emptied her final buckets onto the salt mounds. People were still filling and stitching sacks and heaping them up ready for the camel trains in the morning. At the quartermaster's table, the quartermaster counted the marks next to her name. He nodded to himself. Across one side of his face, the heavy scar looked pinker than yesterday.

"All right," he said. "Two dollars today."

"What?" said Ari. "Come on Wheels, I moved more salt than yesterday."

The quartermaster looked up at her and gave her a sympathetic smile. "Sorry Ari, today's two dollars."

Ari rolled her eyes. "Fine."

She held out her salt covered palm and the quartermaster fumbled in the bag on his desk and took out four half-moon coins, each a dull metallic grey. Dented and chewed, they'd changed hands many times. Ari slipped the precious coins into her trouser pocket.

"Be seein' ya," said the quartermaster.

Ari nodded. "Whatever."

She sulked away, head down. She knew it wasn't the quartermaster's fault. He was all right, one of the good ones. But last year she was making three dollars a day.

There you go making plans again Ari, dreaming of more than your lot. Thinking what you might do with three dollars a day. Earn enough for a camel maybe, or a donkey. But then, where're you gonna go? You gonna go back to the city? Become one of those bottom feeders begging at the gates. They don't open the wall to no one. You could leave Cooper though. Go someplace else.

But, she reminded herself, dreaming is dangerous. First you start at dreaming, then you start at hoping. Before you know it, you're praying to the Maker and you're one step away from total despair.

Ari wasn't one for praying, in this life she looked out for herself. There had to be somewhere better than here though.

She stopped by a stall and picked up a tough flatbread about the size of her fist; one dollar, two half-moon coins. Grain from the city in exchange for the salt. The baker palmed her coins in his big, wiry hands, veins and bones all knotted together. On the counter behind the baker, Ari saw the heap of flatbreads and her stomach groaned for the first time that day, a reminder she'd not yet eaten. She'd toiled all day in the baking sun with nothing to sustain her but a few swallows of the metallic tasting water. Most days it was all she needed. Now she smelt the fresh bread, slightly sweet, slightly sour, and she was starving.

At the well, she refilled her canteen. The well and the salt, that was Cooper; drink the water, sell the salt. She took a long swig and almost choked. As she lowered her canteen again, she watched the sun slip over the horizon and disappear. Gradually, the sky grew a pale pink.

At night, it was safer to hide away. She couldn't afford a safe house, some place they locked at night, so she lived outside of town in one of the many tiny caves that pockmarked the north ridge, forming a discreet diaspora. Here, people kept to themselves.

In the half-light, she made her way down the familiar slope. When she was closer, she saw the tarp, which normally concealed the entrance to her cave, had fallen inwards. Quietly, she placed down her buckets and yoke and drew the make-shift blade she kept sheathed against her ankle.

"I know ya there," she said. "Get outa' 'ere before I send the dog down."

Silence.

Maybe, she thought, the wind had blown open the flap? But that hadn't happened before, and today was no windier than it had been all season. What about an animal? If it was a dingo, it'd already be gone, or else it'd be making a lot more noise. Cautiously, Ari made her way down the hole. It was dark and silent. If someone was there, they were staying mighty quiet.

Carefully, Ari reached around the entrance and retrieved the tiny clay oil lamp she kept close by. She retreated up the hole. She knelt on the ground and, from her pocket, she removed her flint and small metal fire-starter. Two firm strikes and it was lit. Lamp in one hand and blade in the other, she descended back into the hole.

She lived in a cave, just big enough to stand, and long enough to lie down flat on a bed of salt sacks. Lying unconscious on the bed, her hands bound behind her back, was a girl in a long blue dress.

CHAPTER 4

"What the…?"

This hadn't happened before.

Ari glanced back the way she'd come. Darkness had fallen completely and the moon was yet to rise. She scanned the hillside for any sign of a trail, but it was impossible to make out anything.

She turned back to the girl that lay unconscious on the salt sacks.

I gotta think fast, she thought. Otherwise, whoever she is, she'll land us both in trouble.

Ari placed the oil lamp back in its little hole by the entrance. The weak orange glow reflected around the walls of the cave. She rearranged the tarp so that the light wouldn't draw attention.

She looked back at the girl. "What ya doin' 'ere sister?"

The girl didn't stir.

I should drag her outside, she thought. I don't need this, this ain't my problem.

But if the girl didn't wake, the dingoes might get her, or something worse. The dingoes didn't tend to come too close to town, but there were other dangers besides dingoes and this girl looked like she'd already found a few. Besides, it didn't do to go throwing folks out into the desert at night. That wasn't the way. Treat strangers kindly, because you never know when you might be one yourself.

Ari sighed. "Well, ya can't just go droppin' in like this."

With her foot, Ari gave the girl's ribs a gentle prod. There was no response. Ari drew her leg back, ready to kick again, this time harder, but the girl looked so helpless. A memory intruded on Ari's mind, something that had happened long ago. She had been kneeling by a bed. The skin had looked so thin and yellow and she'd seen right through to the bones.

Two things got nothing to do with each other, she thought. And that was all on her.

A small lump formed in Ari's throat.

The girl looked like she'd come from the city; no one around here wore dresses like hers, even one torn and covered with dirt. She looked young, maybe the same age as Ari. Little cuts and bruises blemished her pale skin. Her bare feet were grazed and covered in red dust, her heart-shaped face smeared in blue makeup and dry blood. It had been a long time since Ari had seen anyone wear makeup. The girl had long dark hair that was trying to hold some sort of elaborate shape, but was now failing. On her left temple, the lightly swollen skin was broken and a red stain had seeped into the salt sack beneath. The dress was beautiful; it was long and a deep blue and had a strange shimmering texture.

She's probably an exile, thought Ari. Well, no going back now sister. You crossed the city, now you're just the same as the rest of us.

Ari knelt by the girl.

Maybe I should undo her binds. I guess it seems like the least I can do. That way she might have a fighting chance outside the cave.

The knots were tight and difficult to undo. The thin rope dug into the girl's skin. Ari resorted to using her blade to tug the cords free. She loosened the noose and slid it from the swollen wrists. The hands were small, the fingers fine though they were red and bruised. The sparkly blue lacquer on the chipped nails caught the light of the oil lamp and flickered. Long ago, Ari recalled seeing such things.

The girl stirred. She mumbled quietly, opened her eyes and looked at Ari. She flinched and jerked away.

"Hey, hey," said Ari.

The girl contracted her body into the corner of the cave and stiffened. Her eyes were wide and they fidgeted like those of a scared animal. Even by the dim light of the oil lamp, Ari could see they were a vivid deep blue. The lamplight caught storm-like flecks of cyan and sapphire, swirling around large, dark pupils.

The girl began to shake, breathing in sudden, shallow bursts. She pulled her arms to her chest and inspected her wrists with her fingers, then she pressed frantically at the inside of her left forearm as if she expected something to happen. She paused. Her trembling fingers stretched out across her forearm and she started to scratch it. She looked at Ari.

"Where am I?"

"Just outside Cooper."

"Where's Cooper?"

Ari shrugged. "Dunno. It's Cooper."

"But I mean, where's the city?"

"Depends which way ya go. Right 'ere though, might as well be the other side of the world."

The girl fell silent and dropped her eyes.

Ari scratched at the side of her neck. That was the longest conversation she'd had in a long time. "So," she said, "what ya doin' in my cave?"

The girl looked at Ari and shrugged.

"Look. This is my place right so ya better start answerin' some 'a my questions or ya can take this up with the dingoes eh?"

Wide-eyed, the girl didn't respond.

Ari sighed. "So ya from the city?"

The girl nodded.

"Banished?... Look, ya gonna have to learn some hard lessons if you're set on makin' it out 'ere."

"I want to go back."

"Well you an' me both sister, but ain't gonna happen. No one goes back so ya gonna have to get used to it 'ere. But not right 'ere. This is my place."

The girl's eyes reddened. A blue tear rolled down her cheek. Ari rolled her eyes.

Dag it. How did this happen? What did I do to deserve this tonight?

The girl sniffed.

"Look, ya can't stay 'ere, okay? This is my place. Ya need to move on."

The girl drew her legs to her chest and hugged them. She began to shudder. More blue tears stained her cheeks.

"Dag it," said Ari and slapped her palm against the floor. Her palm stung and she balled up her fingers. The lump in her throat grew.

Ari looked about the cave, avoiding the girl's eyes. She looked at the oil lamp and the plastic bottles full of oil and water she'd wedged into cracks and the bits of broken pottery and coloured beads she'd arranged on tiny rocky shelves. One jagged piece of glazed white porcelain had blue markings that looked like part of a bird.

This girl couldn't stay, that's for sure. She'd have to go find somewhere else to cry. I live alone, no trouble from no one, and I like it that way.

Ari's eyes came to rest on a fuzzy chalk image she'd carefully scraped onto one wall. It was only small. It showed a hut with a chimney with two stick figures standing next to it. She sighed and looked back at the girl.

"Look," she said. "What are ya doin' 'ere?"

The girl gulped heavily. "They took me."

"Who took ya?"

"I don't know. It was my birthday and I wore my favourite dress and I was in the penthouse and they took me and I woke up out here and then some men came and I thought they would kill me and I escaped and now I'm here and I don't even know where here is and I don't know what to do and I just want to go home."

"Sister, I don't even know what ya sayin'."

The girl continued to sob quietly.

"Fine."

Treat strangers kindly, because you never know when you might be one yourself. That's what they say I guess.

Ari found a rag, close to clean, from the pile at the foot of her bed. She took her canteen and emptied a little of the water onto the rag. She crawled over to the girl. Leaning forward, she gently started to clean the wound on the girl's temple. The girl's face and arms were lightly speckled in spots of red.

The girl stopped shuddering and grew quiet.

"So, what do they call ya?"

"Starla," said the girl.

"Starla eh. Well, I'm Ari. Maka knows why I'm tellin' ya that though. So, ya got some place to go? Ya with people? Your people I mean?"

The girl shook her head.

"Well, guess ya kinda lucky to run into the only person in this town who's actually been to Alice."

"Alice?"

"The city. Folks out 'ere, sometimes they call it Alice."

"Why?"

Ari shrugged. "Dunno, don't care. But they do."

"You've been there?"

"Been there, from there."

"How come you're here?"

Ari paused. "Well... Let's save that story for another time eh."

She finished wiping Starla's face and found herself drawn to the long, curved eyelashes.

"Are ya lashes real?"

The right corner of Starla's lip curled subtly upwards. She reached up and pulled one away.

"False."

She pulled away the other and her deep blue eyes were even more vivid.

"Can I?"

Starla held forward the lashes and Ari took them. She inspected them closely in the dim light. They were so delicate and fine and, briefly, she was captivated. She moved them gently with her finger, feeling them tickle her palm.

"You keep them," said Starla.

Ari's cheeks warmed and she grinned. She looked briefly to Starla but couldn't hold her gaze.

"I just didn' see nothin' like that in a long time." She closed her fingers and pocketed the lashes.

"So seriously," said Starla, "how far are we from the city?"

"Well, ya could walk it. It'd take ya days though."

"How many?"

"I dunno, maybe a week. Maybe more."

"Any other way?"

Ari smiled. "Sure, you could drive, but there's no fuel. An' folks who 'ave fuel don't wanna share it. There's old trucks an' things but none of 'em work. Or you could get a camel or a mule but I'm guessin' ya don't have no money?"

Starla shook her head.

"See, I didn't think so. An', well, you can try to earn the money, but trust me sister that'd take ya a hell of a long time."

"You know the way?"

"Sure I do, but you know, it won't do ya any good. No one gets into the city."

"They'll let me in."

"An' what makes ya think that? You're an exile now sister."

"No I'm not, I'm the mayor's daughter."

Ari raised her eyebrows.

"So do you want to get back in?"

"Of course," said Ari. Who didn't wanna get back into the city? Even folks who've never been spend all their days dreaming of getting inside those walls. But most who make the journey still wind up on the outside, taunted by those glittering towers of glass and steel just beyond the wall.

"Well," said Starla, "if you can get me back, I can get you in."

△△△

"So what makes ya think I can get ya back to the city?"

Ari's pale grey eyes had grown wide. Among their whites, angry red blood vessels formed like the lines of a map. Deep creases folded around her dark eyelids and the muscles in her cheeks tensed as if she was about to squint.

"You can," said Starla. "You know the way. It's a simple exchange, you get me back, I get you in."

"An' they'll let me in?"

"Of course they will, I'm the mayor's daughter. I'm one of the most important people in the city."

Even if she wanted to, Starla had no idea if she could get this girl into the city, but right now that wasn't important. Right now she needed to get back by any means necessary. And once close enough to the city walls, she could call inside using the telephone implanted in her left arm. As soon as her hands were free, she'd pressed her fingers to the skin, but nothing had happened. She was probably too far from the city.

When I'm closer it'll work, Starla assured

herself.

At first, Starla had been shocked to find herself in this cave and with this strange girl. It had taken all her effort to stop herself shaking and she was already ashamed of how she'd acted. When the tears came, she wasn't even sure why she was crying. It was as if she'd been outside her body, looking down on herself and telling herself to calm down. Come on Starla she'd said, you are better than this, you have to take control of yourself. Now, the earlier events of the day were a blur; a jumble of events and images that all seemed far away and to have happened to someone else. Now, there was nothing she could do except endeavour to resolve the situation.

I am Starla Corinth, first daughter of the city. I am my father's daughter.

She scratched absently at the inside of her arm. Her skin felt strangely numb.

You can do this Starla, she told herself. You can get yourself back to the city.

Smoke collected around the low roof of the cave. The oil lamp released a rich, fatty smell. Ari scratched the grubby side of her neck. She looked like she was starving. She was stick thin, her skin blotchy and dark. Her hair, shaved close to the scalp, left her almost bald.

She probably has lice, thought Starla. The cave was probably crawling with them. That's probably why I'm scratching. A hot, prickly shiver crawled over Starla's skin.

But I need her. She's essential to the plan. This girl has value. And she's from the city, she's not an outsider. Maybe I can trust her?

Like you could really trust anyone in the city Starla.

But maybe I can?

And she doesn't look sick, she doesn't look mutated. Maybe the cave is safe? But what if she's a carrier? But she can't be, she says she's from the city. She'd be dead by now if it wasn't safe.

"So," said Starla, "do we have a deal?"

Ari toyed with her fingers. Her hands were dry and calloused but they looked strong, like this girl knew how to survive. Her nails were ragged and a large, dark blood blister had formed under her left thumbnail. She sucked on the corner of her lower lip. Starla found it impossible to tell her age.

"Ya know it'll be dangerous."

"Honestly, the day I'm having, I really don't doubt it."

"Thing is, I leave 'ere, I go with you, I gotta cash in. There's no work for me at the city walls. Either I'm in the city or I walk. It was a hell of a journey to get 'ere an' I ain't goin' back unless I get in. Do ya see?"

"Look," said Starla. "You seem like a reasonable person. You're from the city, you don't belong here. Neither of us do. Now, either you can stay here, and live in your hole in the ground, and do whatever it is you do with your days. Or, you can come with me?"

She's tempted, thought Starla. But is she tempted enough?

"Would it help if I said please?"

Starla's heart started to beat faster again. She thought of the dark wasteland outside. She'd no idea what time it was. Her skin began to prickle and the muscles around her spine tightened.

What if she won't help.

Starla's hands began to shiver again.

What's wrong with me? I need to think straight.

Ari sucked again at the corner of her lip.

"Well?"

Ari sighed. "Okay." She shook her head and grinned. "Well okay, I'm in."

I have her. "We have a trade?"

"We have a trade."

I've a plan, thought Starla, or something at least.

"It's gonna be a long walk," said Ari.

"I understand."

"An' ya gonna need some proper clothes."

Starla looked down at her now ruined dress. "Yes, I guess."

"We're gonna need a plan," said Ari.

"We leave tomorrow?"

"Maybe. We need supplies. Water, food, clothing. Ya know I'm gonna have to cash in all my dollars for this."

"They're useless in the city anyway."

"Yeah, well, it's taken me a long while to make 'em."

Starla sighed. "I'm sorry you'll need to spend your money."

"No worries. Look, if we're doin' this we're doin' this."

"So we follow the road?"

Ari shook her head. "Too dangerous. Road's too busy; full of camel trains an' whatever else. An' when ya sleepin' at night, more 'an likely you'll get ya neck slit or worse. No, we go cross-country. Faster on foot anyhow. Shorter. We'll have to cross the swamp but that's okay. Better n' the road anyhow."

Starla smiled inwardly. Trade or no trade, this girl was getting her back to the city.

CHAPTER 5

Ari kept all her half-moon dollar coins in an old pot hidden out of sight behind a rock in the cave. She wasn't sure how long she'd been collecting the coins, whenever she didn't need to spend them, and she wasn't so good at counting, but she'd a reasonable number of them now. Enough, hopefully, for what they needed.

That night Starla slept fitfully on some of Ari's old salt sacks. In the cool darkness, Ari could hear Starla murmuring and rolling around on the hard floor beside her. Ari had shared her bread with Starla and Starla had struggled to swallow it. It wasn't what she was used to but there weren't any syntho cubes out here. "Is there nothing else?" Starla had pleaded, and Ari had to tell her this was all she had. Sometime in the night, Starla had awoken, doubled over, and clambered out of the hole. From inside the cave, Ari could hear her retching. Starla stayed outside for a while and Ari lay in the darkness, waiting for her to return or to hear the dingoes. Eventually Starla returned to the cave and sat down on the floor beside Ari.

Ari pretended to sleep, but her mind raced with images of a lost life in the city. She remembered the myriad of coloured lights reflecting on her bedroom wall. She remembered the feel of the soft, crisp blankets, tucked tightly around her. She remembered the interwoven pattern of the carpet and the smooth, endless surfaces of walls and doors and tables. She remembered not being hungry, a life without that perpetual, hollow emptiness in her gut. With these images, she drifted closer to sleep, lying on the rough material of the salt sack, her stomach starting to grumble. She never knew if Starla lay down again.

△△△

After dawn, Ari gathered what few things she owned of value. Some she would keep for the journey, like the fire-starter and flint, her blade, the canteen; others she'd trade, like the oil lamp and oil. She'd trade the oil but fill the plastic bottle that held it with water.

"We'll have to getcha somethin' else to wear," said Ari. "An' somethin' for ya head."

"Why?"

"You're not used to the sun. Ya won't make it a day like that."

Starla's pale skin looked like it'd never seen the sun.

She won't make it an hour, thought Ari. Not without my help and maybe not even then.

Doubt crept into Ari's mind.

For this, I sacrifice everything; if Starla dies in the desert then it will all be for nothing.

For the first part of the journey, she'd have to carry on her back everything they'd need. Out on the plains, there wasn't much of anything but the red dust, and Starla couldn't carry much. And they'd have to avoid the tribesmen. Ari had heard stories about the tribesmen, stories she didn't want to think about now.

She pulled at the seam of her pocket and felt the weight of her hard-earned coins. All those days spent toiling on the salt plains.

Am I too quick to leave this place? But how many years has it been Ari? How many seasons?

Until yesterday, returning was an impossible dream. She was an exile. Now there was hope.

△△△

While Ari went into Cooper, Starla stayed hidden in the cave. She'd barely slept. For a short while she'd dozed, curled up on the hard stone floor; in her dreams, faceless attackers had chased her through the brightly lit streets of the city. She'd tried to find help, but the people she encountered ignored her pleas. Finally, she'd made it to the footbridge that crossed the Todd River. Now her legs were heavy and crossing the bridge was like wading through a heavy current. By halfway, she was on her knees, unable to move any further forward. Her body shook. Beneath her, the bridge began to flex and shudder. It had become a dam, holding back a great body of water, pooled on one side. The metal structure creaked painfully and tore open, sending her tumbling downwards.

Starla had struck the surface but found herself sinking in a thick, red quicksand. She was out in the wasteland, her eyes straining against the harsh light. She clutched handfuls of sand, but it slipped through her fingers and still she sank. She was up to her waist, then her shoulders, then her neck. She struggled frantically. She tried to cry out but no sound came. The sand poured into her mouth, her ears, up her nostrils. It was up to her eyes. She couldn't breathe. The empty world prepared to swallow her.

Starla had awoken startled. She'd sat up and doubled over, a round pain in her stomach. She'd crawled out of the hole, fallen to her knees and vomited.

It was dark and silent outside the cave. The jagged shapes of rocks and the low hill leading up from the cave were just discernible in the thin moonlight. Starla inhaled deep lungfuls of the cool air. Sweat poured from her clammy skin. For a while she sat, bent over, nursing her stomach.

I must get home, she'd told herself. I should be there now; I shouldn't be here. None of this makes any sense. Maybe I'm getting sick?

Headaches, nausea, vomiting.

Her head thumped. She shivered and began to scratch the inside of her arm.

This is all a mistake. I'll be rescued soon. They'll find me somehow. But no one ever leaves the city Starla. No one leaves and no one returns. But I'm the mayor's daughter, they'll have to come for me. Won't they?

Not if you're infected Starla.

Finally, Starla had crawled back down into the hole and sat down next to Ari. In the darkness, she'd seen the sickening look in the old man's eyes as he'd licked his lips and inched towards her. Her heart began to race.

She could smell his sour stench; she could smell it all over herself; acidic and rotten. She wanted to scrub her skin clean and she scratched again at the inside of her arm. She felt the small welts coming up where she'd been scratching. Red blisters. She tried to inspect her arm, but in the pitch darkness, she couldn't make out anything.

The old man licked his lips, gloating, his black eyes wide.

Starla had shut her eyes tight and willed the image away. Instead, she'd seen the glimpses of red wasteland through the dusty windows. Her skin had begun to prickle. Night had fallen and she wasn't home. Her gut twisted. She was trapped outside the wall.

Starla shivered in the cave. She was alone now. A thin daylight intruded around the tarp. The air was heavy but Starla feared leaving the cave alone. Her head swam, her face hot, and it hurt every time she swallowed. Red marks had formed on the inside of her arm.

Why has this happened to me? This isn't fair. I must be dreaming. This is all some terrible nightmare and soon I will wake. Perhaps I've gone mad? Perhaps I've not left the city at all, but instead I'm trapped in some kind of asylum. Is all of this some kind of elaborate fantasy, conjured from years spent staring out across the wall and into the wasteland?

But the cave seemed all too real.

She inhaled slowly, letting the stale air of the cave fill her lungs. She could still smell the fatty scent of the oil lamp.

Maybe I should be going into town and seeking help there?

But it was too dangerous. Now, every time she closed her eyes, she saw the old man licking his lips and inching closer.

She flexed out her fingers, feeling the tendons stretch.

I am Starla Corinth, first daughter of the city. I cannot show weakness. When the outsider returns, I will take control of this situation.

△△△

In the bazaar, Ari traded the oil and the lamp for more plastic bottles and she sold her buckets and yoke for a few extra coins.

Even early, the market thronged. Stalls pressed together along narrow streets. Strung overhead between the buildings, threadbare canvases shaded the walls from the heavy sun. The air was thick and humid. Sellers of clothing and food found their places next to counters piled high with bits of scavenged metal, or plastic of every shape and colour, its original purpose long forgotten. Troves of it was pulled from the desert and hauled into town on camels, yet much of it was worthless. There were counters full of rusty keys to long forgotten doors, the shells of clocks whose innards were repurposed and forgotten, and books that Ari couldn't read with splitting spines and faded, yellow pages now crumbling to dust. Ironmongers worked in the street, shaping tools and hammering at bits of old machinery that might pump up water or work a pulley in a mine. Or they were making carts from junk with rubber wheels, to haul down to the salt plains or to hitch to a donkey.

Between the traders and customers pressed the big fella's men, recognisable by their red armbands and the large, heavy looking guns they carried. They were meant to keep the peace, but no one wanted to catch their attention. These were the people you paid for protection, and the people you needed protecting from. They collected debts you didn't know you owed, sometimes in money, more often in blood. People disappeared; they never came back. If they were alive, they were probably in the ore mines.

Ari spent some of her half-moon coins on bread and a little kangaroo jerky. For Starla, she bought a canteen with a shoulder strap, a shirt, trousers, a jumper, a shawl for her head and an old pair of boots she hoped would fit.

At the back of the bazaar, in an open paddock, worked the animal seller. A few donkeys and camels pressed against the walls, their heads drooping, their matted bodies all skin and bone. With the last of her coins, Ari bought a dog on a cord. It with a little grey mongrel with a scrawny body and a pointed snout. It wasn't too fidgety and Ari thought it looked like it could take care of itself. It'd be their best shot at keeping back the dingoes.

When Ari got back to the cave she found Starla hiding in the darkness, her eyes wide. For a moment, she looked like she didn't recognise Ari. Her skin was slick with sweat and she shivered slightly. She looked so pale, even compared with earlier.

"Ya gotta drink sister." Ari handed her a canteen. "That one's yours."

Starla took it and gulped heavily then choked. "That tastes horrible."

"Well, ya welcome. Here, put these on."

Starla inspected the garments that Ari had

acquired. She wrinkled her nose.

"Look, ya not gettin' anywhere in that dress. We got a long way to walk. Now I don't really care what ya wear but ya gotta get me in the city right?" Ari placed the boots down next to Starla. "And ya gonna need footwear too."

Ari looked away. She heard rustling and when she turned back Starla had changed. Starla held forward the boots.

"These are too big."

Ari rolled her eyes. Taking her blade, and before Starla could protest, Ari cut a strip of fabric from Starla's dress.

"Here, stuff that in the toe."

Starla looked like she might protest at the further damage to her dress, but she did as Ari said.

Ari held out a piece of cord. "For ya hair."

Ari rolled up some of the salt sacks that had made her bed in the cave. They would need them at night. She used one to contain the others and stuffed in her own jumper and all the plastic bottles. They would need plenty of water. She added the bread and the little jerky. She slipped the fire-starter and flint in her pocket; the blade was in its sheath on her ankle.

Starla fidgeted with her new clothes. Dark rings had formed under her eyes, which now looked a paler shade of blue than before, and her skin was clammy and grey. Ari took Starla's jumper and pushed it into the sack. After a second thought, she added the tattered blue dress. She looked at the coloured beads and bits of broken pottery she'd gradually collected.

I don't need them, she thought. That junk will only weigh us down.

The jagged piece of glazed white porcelain showing part of the blue bird sat on its little rocky shelf. She reached for it, then hesitated, and drew her hand away.

She took one last look at the chalk image on the wall with the two stick figures.

This stuff only ever weighs me down.

When they got outside the cave, Ari dragging the bag, Starla saw the dog sitting patiently by the entrance.

"Hey, what's this dog?"

"He's ours, he's comin' with us."

"You have a dog?"

"Got a dog."

Starla knelt down and stroked its head. "What's his name?"

"He ain't got none."

"He should have a name."

Ari rolled her eyes. "He's a workin' dog, keepin' away the dingoes."

Starla looked at Ari. "Well, he should still have a name."

"He's called dog, right, ya wanna call him anythin' else then ya go ahead."

Starla looked back at the dog. It tipped its head to the side and pricked its ear. With both hands, she cupped his head. The dog didn't seem to mind.

"Well, I'm sure I'll think of something."

"Great," said Ari, "well you take 'is cord then."

Ari lumbered the bag onto her back with two cords she'd use for straps. Starla took the dog's lead, canteen over her shoulder. They stopped by the well and filled their water bottles and canteens, and then they were moving, away from Cooper and away from Ari's hole in the ground.

Ari paused and took one brief look back, spying the spot that for so long she'd called home, and her limbs felt oddly heavy. There was the little dip in the rocks; the tarp covering the entrance made it all but invisible.

Maybe I'll be back?

She thought of the beads and the bits of broken pottery, sitting where she'd left them, and the chalk figures. Had she deliberately left these items behind, preserving some kind of home she could always return to? You could hate a place for so long, and yet when the day comes to leave it, you miss it before you've even gone. And Starla, already so weak, would she really make it?

Ari chewed on her bottom lip, a hollow feeling growing in her stomach. She thought of the long, hard days toiling on the salt plains, and the cold nights shivering alone in a cave; the feeling of barely being alive at all. Then she thought of the city, hovering in her mind's eye like a shimmering mirage, forever slightly out of focus. Could she still remember the layout of that apartment? Was her room still there, to find again? Sealed all these years, awaiting her return.

The cave, Cooper; these things will only hold you down Ari. So good riddance to it all. I ain't never coming back.

But still, the hollow feeling nagged her.

CHAPTER 6

"Starla, I don't know why you love this place so." Liviana Panache toyed with her fingers. "It smells."

"You didn't have to come here," replied Starla. "It was your choice."

"Yes," said Liviana absently. Today, Liviana was so blonde her hair was almost white. Tonight she might be something else, but today she was blonde. These erratic transformations complimented her personality. Liviana would try to be many things, yet wound up archiving none of them.

The grey koala clung to the ash white trunk with its six fingers and four thumbs. Its lazy black eyes, like two glass spheres, were half closed. One of its bushy ears twitched.

The koala didn't do anything, it never did. Koalas spent their lives asleep.

Just like me, thought Starla.

They don't go anywhere except here or there, and here might as well be there. Starla liked bringing Liviana to the koala enclosure, she suspected the creatures bored Liviana more than the rest of the animals. The lions and tigers prowled back and forth, the monkeys chattered and leaped from tree to tree, but the koalas stayed were they were. Perhaps they, better than the other animals, understood the true nature of the zoo. There was nowhere else to go.

"You know that guard's been watching us," said Liviana.

"They're always watching us."

The koala slowly blinked. For a moment, Starla thought it was about to yawn. Gradually, its pink lips parted, but then it seemed to think better of it.

"Not like that guard," said Liviana. "He's been staring right at you."

"What guard?"

"By the pavilion."

As Starla looked up, the guard looked away. He was young, with sandy blonde hair, and wore the crisp, light blue uniform of the praetorian guard.

The guards weren't meant to stare. They were always there, but they weren't meant to stare.

"Maybe he's got a thing for you? You should report him."

"I guess," said Starla, as she turned back to

the koala enclosure and the guard faded from her mind.

△△△

They said nothing for a long time after leaving Cooper and this suited Ari. Starla covered her head with the shawl and held the lead of the dog loosely. The dog walked obediently at her heels. Ahead, the land shimmered in a hot haze. At first the ground was rocky, as it was around Cooper, but gradually it gave way to an endless red dust, flat and featureless to the horizon.

They followed a trail out to the old railway line. Twisted and bowed, the metal tracks had warped under the blistering sun. Beneath the rolling dust, sections of the line disappeared entirely, only to reappear further along the trail. Here and there, the concrete sleepers were just visible.

"Who built this?" asked Starla.

Ari shrugged. "Dunno. But we follow it."

"It goes to the city?"

"Maybe once. Now it only takes us part way. It don' cut through the swamp see. It goes another way."

They followed the tracks north. The landscape was eerily silent, with only the sound of the wind working its way across the flat emptiness to interrupt their thoughts. Ari thought of the town of Cooper, perhaps she'd grown more used to the place than she'd realised. The steady work, the bread and water, a place to rest her head. Routine can go a long way to making a place a home. And out here, the mind played tricks. There wasn't enough to see, so the mind drew its own pictures. Ari thought of the Angu woman she'd seen yesterday, bent over, working the salt with a pickaxe. She'd be there now, filling her buckets. She'd be there tomorrow too, and the day that followed, and the day after that. At dusk she'd make her way to Wheels who would be sitting in his wheelchair in the shade and he'd hand her a few more half-moon coins. Maybe one or two less than he had the year before.

Digging the salt, filling the buckets; one more foot in front of the other, eyes on the tracks as they cut through the emptiness. Today is a day, just as yesterday and the one that came before.

Would Wheels wonder where I am today?

Starla took a long swig from her canteen.

"Careful with the water," said Ari. "No water out 'ere. What we got, it's gotta last us a while."

"There's no more wells?"

"Nope. Not this way. Maybe a billabong if we're lucky an' it's not dry, but until the swamp we just gotta make what we got."

It ain't rained in a long time, thought Ari, and no sign it will anytime soon.

There were no thunderheads on the horizon, just a pale blue sky that met a shimmering flat line at the edge of the world.

Ari wiped the sweat from her shaved head, inhaled deeply, and licked her dry lips. No salt out here at least. She was used to this; she didn't need much water. This wasn't so for Starla; she'd need more rations and Ari carried far more water than she alone needed. Enough, hopefully, for Starla. Their destinies were bound, and there was no going back on this one. Ari had made this journey twice before. It was third time lucky, she wasn't doing this again.

They trudged onwards in silence. Further down the tracks, the foot-high remains of a building protruded out of the dust. On the tracks, on six sets of metal wheels, sat a huge piece of rusting machinery. A twisted panel on its side bowed open exposing metal bowels like the innards of some mechanised beast. The wind whispered around its many surfaces, blowing wisps of red dust into the air. Further on along the tracks sat a strange marker; a cross attached to a bent metal pole. On either side, a vague trail was just visible, running at right angles in either direction from the railway.

Ari and Starla pushed on, following the metal tracks through the red dust.

△△△

The silence deafened Starla. Ahead, clouds of red dust rolled over the tracks.

Starla couldn't remember ever being anywhere so quiet. Her heart skipped quickly and the walls around her chest felt thin. She could hear blood pumping around her eardrums, along with the slightest high-pitched ring of tinnitus. She listened to the crunch of the dry dirt underfoot. Her ill-fitting boots pinched and rubbed; her foot tripped on a stone and she almost lost her balance. Her eyes teared and, with the back of her hand, she tried to wipe away the grit. Through the blur, she watched the gently swaying figure of Ari.

She thinks she's better than me.

Starla heard it in the tone of Ari's voice and in the way she gave her orders. She watched the back of Ari's exposed neck; her shaved head gently swayed and gleamed in the sunlight.

She doesn't know her station. But you need her Starla.

It took all Starla's efforts to maintain normal discourse with the girl. Her head now spun and thoughts and ideas were blurring together. When she closed her eyes, she saw the old man licking his lips.

"He said she's worth something."

That's what the other man had said. She remembered the gun, pressed up against the old man's temple, and her heartbeat ringing in her ears and the sour stench of the old man's breath. Now she was out in the open, she wanted to hide, to squeeze into some tiny crack and stay there until this was all over. She wanted to be back in the cave. She longed for protective surfaces to squeeze around her. Instead, there was only the red dust and the long abandoned tracks.

Starla remembered the paintings in the city archive. Lush fields, green valleys, waterfalls.

How, she wondered, could I have ever wanted to leave the city? How could I ever imagine the outside as anything but this?

Starla's tacky skin itched. She longed to dive into clear water

She studied the back of Ari's neck. She wanted to leap out and strangle her, to squeeze out the life, to take back control of this hideous situation.

Why did I let her bring me here? This is all her fault. The more I think on it, the more I see it. I should abandon her.

But, then I'd be alone. Alone and sick.

I hate this girl. How dare she make me feel this helpless?

She closed her eyes and saw Max grinning. That sideways grin, as if one side of his face disagreed with the other. "To hell with them all." That's what he'd said.

Father, Liviana, the whole lot of them. I wish Max would come and save me. Prove himself worthy. That would be better than this. Then maybe I'd reconsider?

She saw her fish, swimming in its bowl of water, its bulbous eyes peering up at her. Her mouth salivated.

Starla opened her canteen and took a swig of water. It tasted metallic. Little white stars formed across her vision. She tightened her grip on the cord.

Am I leading the dog or is the dog leading me? Either way, he should have a name. Why did I never name the fish?

Starla's heart was pounding. Her vision blurred and she tried again to concentrate on the skinny figure of Ari, moving further ahead now, the bulky sack on her back wobbling from side to side. Starla stumbled, her feet twisting in the boots. She was so sleepy.

Starla's head began to swim. She stopped walking and, for a moment, was quite happy to watch the figure of Ari separate into two distinct forms. The world seemed to be tipping upside down.

△△△

Starla collapsed and the dog barked.

CHAPTER 7

There was nothing to burn on the dust plains. It would be a cold, dark night by the tracks.

Ari spared a little water to moisten Starla's forehead and lips. She laid out the salt sacks on the ground in the approximation of two beds; a sack each to lie on and another to sleep under. She used Starla's rolled up dress as a pillow for her head and moved her onto her bed. Ari wasn't sure the dog was ready to be let off its lead, she didn't want it to go running back to Cooper, and so she tied the cord to her wrist. Lying on her bed, Starla murmured occasionally but didn't really become conscious until the big red sun was setting over the horizon and the air began to grow cool.

"Here, put this on," said Ari, offering the jumper.

"What happened?"

"Ya collapsed. It's the heat."

"My head hurts."

"Ya need to eat, ya need water, and ya need to sleep. We're gonna stay 'ere tonight."

Ari tore one of the pieces of flatbread in half and then broke away a bit of the jerky.

"Here, eat these. Ya have to eat."

"This all we got."

"No, I'm hidin' the syntho cubes. Yeah, it's all we got."

Little miss ungrateful, thought Ari, don't she know how hard food is to come by here? But, she'll get you into the city. This girl just needs to wise up, that's all.

She took the other half of the flatbread and began chewing on it hungrily. She gulped it down with a swig of water and it tasted good.

Starla took the bread and jerky. She chewed unhappily on the bread.

"Drink some water too or ya gonna die out 'ere."

Starla did what she was told.

The dog had been lying on the ground since Ari had made camp but now it sat up and gazed with concentration at the horizon. It sniffed at the air and then it froze completely, its ears pricked.

"What's with the dog?" asked Starla.

"It knows somethin's out there."

"What's there?"

"The dingoes."

"What's the dingoes anyway?"

Ari smiled painfully. "They're about the

most dangerous thin' out 'ere. Not really a problem in the day but at night. They'll snatch ya right up while ya sleep. An' we ain't got much chance if they attack."

"But we got the dog."

"Yeah, mutt 'ere wouldn't be much cop in a fight with one but the dingoes don't like other dogs see. It should keep 'em away. That's why it's workin' for its keep."

Starla took the jerky and held it out to the dog, who without argument swallowed it whole.

"What the hell ya doin'?" said Ari.

"He needs to eat."

"Like hell it does. Ya know how little we got of that? Dog can find its own food."

"Not tied up he can't."

"It can an' it will. Don't ya worry about it sister. Dog knows what to do 'ere better 'an you. An' dog don't need to eat every day, you do. Dag it, Starla."

Ari kicked at the dust. This girl really needed to wise up. They didn't have enough food to start feeding dogs. She hunkered down onto her salt sack, dragging the dog on its lead, and pulled the other sack over her. She lay back and looked up to the sky. Stars like tiny embers had started to appear; little points of light that even night couldn't snuff out. Her eyes lingered on the Maker star, motionless above. The others moved, but not the Maker star. It looked right down at you, seeing all you did, for good or bad.

Ari heard Starla pull over her salt sack and sniff.

"Get some sleep sister."

Starla said nothing and for a time they both lay in silence. Still the dog sat upright, looking to the horizon, barely moving, occasionally sniffing the air. The big moon rose overhead and the world was bathed in a silver glow.

A low whining howl broke the silence. It sounded quiet and far away. Then another joined it.

The night song of the dingoes; make sure tonight it's not for you.

Ari shivered under her salt sack and hugged herself closer.

Starla whispered, "Those the dingoes?"

"Yeah," said Ari. "Those are the dingoes."

CHAPTER 8

"I understand you were outside without an escort again," her father said. She couldn't see his face, hidden in the shadows of her bedroom. It was late. He sat in a chair at the end of her bed, his head bowed, one hand playing with his chin. Starla sat up in bed.

"My dear, what if you had been abducted?"

Starla awakened and wondered where she was. Remembering, she pulled the salt sack closer and shivered. Her head hurt and her stomach grumbled. She remembered the old man licking his lips and she shuddered and was no longer hungry. She scrunched up her body, hugged her knees, and lay there a long time.

The following morning, as soon as the sun was up, Ari started packing up the camp. Starla sat on a rail, holding the lead of the dog, and chewed unhappily at a bit of the jerky. It tasted of salt, it stuck in her throat, and it made her thirstier.

"What is this stuff?" asked Starla.

Ari shrugged and stuffed one salt sack into another. "Kangaroo I think."

Starla spat the meat onto the ground and grimaced. "It's animals?"

The dog dipped its head and licked up the partly chewed jerky.

"Yeah, what did ya think it was? Could be camel or even dingo of course."

Bile rose in Starla's throat. She leant over the rail and retched emptily. Her throat hurt and her head spun.

Ari rolled up the jumpers and the dress and stuffed them into the sack.

"Ya gonna 'ave to eat somethin' proper soon," she said.

Starla looked at the dog. He looked back at her with kindly eyes and tipped his head. Today he seemed calm and alert, unconcerned with the dingoes that last night he'd listened for so intently. Starla had also listened to the howls; they'd sounded remote and lonely, and far away. Starla ruffled the bristly fur on the top of his head.

"I'm not going to eat animals."

"Well, dunno what else ya gonna eat out 'ere. Bread'll be finished soon."

They continued their journey in silence. Ari walked ahead, carrying the bag, Starla stumbled behind, the dog at her heels. She dragged her aching limbs, the balls of her feat throbbed. The world looked the same, a vast unchanging emptiness.

Frequently, she took big swigs from her canteen. Her moist clothes stuck to her tacky skin. Starla had refilled her canteen that morning, and when, sometime later, she finally broke the silence to ask for more water, all Ari could say was, "Already?" But Ari stopped, and Starla sat down on the rail while Ari refilled the canteen.

"Do we follow these tracks much further?" asked Starla.

Ari paused and looked each way. "I dunno." She took a swig from her canteen. "I'll know it when I see it."

Sometime later, they came across a dusty collection of discarded items spread carelessly across their path. Initially, Starla didn't recognise what she was looking at. She followed the knobbly ends of long, sweeping femurs to a prickly, snake-like vertebrae; images from a school lesson only half absorbed. The collapsed ribcage looked like it might have once housed an ornamental bird that had long escaped through the broken bars. Finally, her eyes met the smooth, bald skull, the jaw half buried in the red dust, the eye sockets hollow and empty. A shiver ran down her spine.

"Is that a person?"

"Yeah," said Ari. "That's a fella all right. I reckon he's felt better though."

Picked dry, its yellow bones exposed and explored, little bits of fabric still clung between its joints. The dog sniffed a fibula.

"An' that'll be us if we're not careful," added Ari. "Ya can go for days out 'ere without seein' no one."

A chill crept across Starla's heart.

I might die out here.

When the thought came, it was sudden. Even when she'd had the gun pointed at her head, she hadn't really considered the true possibility of her demise.

How could such a thing ever happen to me? Not here, not now. Not to Starla Corinth, first daughter of the city. Death was something for other people.

But death stretched out before her on the dusty ground and she knew it wasn't a monster under her bed or a gun pointed at her head; death was its own horror. Out here, all you had to do was lie down and die; death required nothing more.

An acidic bile burnt the back of Starla's throat and she thought she was going to retch.

She fought the feeling.

Even face down, the skull seemed to be grimacing at her, or maybe it was laughing, taunting her sudden fear.

Hey Starla, do you not see I'm your future? This is your fate. Did no one tell you how utterly stupid you were to put all your trust in this person from the outside? This walking disease. And now, she's dragged you all the way out into the middle of the wasteland. Out here, you will die. At least back in Cooper there were other people; here there is nothing and no one. This place is a grave-yard. This is where people go to die. And not just people, you Starla. This bald headed girl, she's the angel of death.

"He ain't gonna bite," said Ari.

Starla looked up and saw the contours of Ari's skull with her shaven scalp, almost bald, the taut cheekbones and sunken eyes, so pale and grey, and her thin lips drawn across her jaw. She was as skel-etal as the bone structure lying face down in the dust.

Starla started to shake.

"Ya know sister," said Ari. "We'll be right."

Ari gave Starla a little smile; to Starla she looked like the reaper. The smile was unconvin-cing, almost a leer. Ari turned and walked on. Eventually Starla followed, half lost in a dream.

Face down in the dust, the endoskeleton formed a permanent reminder for those that walked the trail. Beside these forgotten tracks lay the everlasting price of failure.

△△△

Finally, in the late afternoon, the landscape began to change. An outline of lumpy shapes formed along the horizon, and soon these became rocks and boulders. Smooth and rusty red, Starla wel-comed these new features. In the endless white-washed world of the dust plains, with little to focus on, her eyes had begun to strain.

When the sun started to set and the sky began to turn pink, Ari dropped the bag on the ground and started making camp. She spread out the bags, emptying the contents onto the ground, and said, "Ya can let the dog off the cord now."

"He's not going to run?"

"I don't think so, it's gotten used to us now."

Starla sat down on her sack and undid the cord. As soon as he was free, the dog trotted off over the rocks out of sight. Starla sank her face into her hands. Her head thumped. In the darkness behind her eyelids, she saw the skull grin at her.

You'll die out here Starla. This place is a graveyard.

The skull licked its lips. Starla smelt the foul stench of its breath.

No, she told herself, I am my father's daughter. I can do this. I will not die out here.

She pressed her palms into the rolling balls of her eyes.

I'm stronger than this. I'm stronger than this girl I'm shackled to. She's a means to an end. I will survive this.

I just wish my head would stop thumping.

Still the skull grinned at her, its hollow eye sockets so like Ari's.

Then Ari said, "I think someone's followin' us."

CHAPTER 9

Ari set out up the rock face. On the smooth surface, her boots slipped and she had to use her
hands to steady herself. At the top, she shielded
her eyes from the dying sun and followed the
tracks south. In the middle distance, a thin column of dark smoke trickled upwards. Ari sighed.

Dag it.

There were two options; either someone else
was travelling this way, or they were being followed. Neither was good news; in Ari's experience people were almost always trouble, whether
people from Cooper or tribesmen. Whoever it
was, at least they were camped for the night.
They must be travelling with stuff to burn. Maybe
they'll be slower? But, maybe they had vehicles.

Ari looked down towards the camp where
Starla sat on her sack, bent over with her head in
her hands. She was suffering; this was bad. Starla
couldn't go on, she had to rest. And they didn't

have enough food or water. She'd miscalculated their provisions. They were almost out of water already. Ari knew she'd be fine, but for someone who had never left the city? And already Starla looked bad. She looked pale, she wasn't walking straight and her eyes were getting that distant look, what people sometimes called the dust blindness. She was dying out here and they'd only been walking two days. They had a long way to go yet. Whoever these people were behind them, Starla would never outrun them.

Ari slipped down the rock face and walked back over to the camp.

"Ya know any reason folks would be followin' us?"

Starla shook her head, her face still in her hands.

Ari knelt down. "You said ya were abducted. Ya know who by?"

Again Starla shook her head.

Ari sighed. "No idea at all?"

Starla lifted her head. "My abductors were attacked. There was this argument, something about the big fellow."

Ari raised her eyebrows. "The Big Fella?"

"I think." Starla dropped her head back into her hands.

"The Big Fella," Ari repeated. If he was after them then he meant business. He had resources; guns, animals, maybe even vehicles. And this girl was the mayor's daughter.

"I guess ya didn't think to mention this be-fore?"

Starla shook her head.

Dag it, thought Ari. I really thought we had a chance, but with the big fella on our trail?

This was trouble. Ari had no idea how much trouble but she knew it was trouble. In Cooper she'd known enough about the big fella to avoid ever getting in his way.

And while they're about it, she thought, they'll either kill me or send me to the ore mines.

Ari wasn't sure which was worse.

At least we're ahead, she thought, for now. But depending on how they're moving, they could catch up with us pretty quick. We don't have the time to stop and camp. We need to push on. They might have animals or even a truck.

Out from the rocks appeared the dog. He trotted over, the tail of a lizard hanging from his mouth.

Ari studied the rocks.

If they have vehicles, they won't get over those. And on the rocks we wouldn't leave tracks. Can dogs pick up a scent? Don't they need some-thing to follow? How should I know? Maybe they won't have dogs? They'll have weapons and ammo, they won't need dogs.

"All right," said Ari. "We can't stay 'ere long. We rest an' when the moon's up we move again."

"More walking?"

Ari shook her head. "Now we climb."

CHAPTER 10

Once the moon was up, Ari roused Starla.

"Come on," she said. "We can rest later. We 'ave to get away from the tracks."

Ari didn't bother putting the dog back on its lead. It seemed to be sticking with them anyway. Far away, she could hear the dingoes mournful song.

Just another thing tracking us, she thought. Well, the dog'll keep them off us.

Moonlight outlined the dark shapes of the rocks. The dog bounded ahead, but Ari was more cautious as she clambered onto the first ledge. She turned and held out her hand to Starla. Starla's eyes glinted in the moonlight. Ari hauled her up.

In the darkness, they worked their way from one outcrop to the next, mindful of the perilous crevices. Ari shivered. It wasn't the height that worried her, it was the falling. A height was nothing to be scared of, but you'd have to be crazy not to be worried about falling ten foot down and breaking your neck.

At some point, Starla fell. She cried out. Looking down, Ari saw a dark shape moving between the rocks.

"Please," said Starla.

Ari felt around the side of the rock until her fingers found Starla's. She gripped her hand and pulled her up. Her shoulder strained. When Ari straightened, she felt faint.

"Ya gotta be more careful sister."

Starla clung to the smooth surface of the rock. "I'm trying."

When dawn broke, Ari found a shaded spot under a rock and they both lay down underneath. Ari refilled their canteens and they both took long gulps, then Starla fell asleep while Ari watched the sun climb higher. If people were following, then they'd see the trail dry up. They'd know they'd taken to the rocks, but they wouldn't know where. We could be under any rock here. That, she considered, would have to do.

She was utterly exhausted.

△△△

When Starla awoke, the sun was high and both Ari and the dog were sleeping soundly in the shade. It was hot, but bearable. Lying here was almost comfortable.

Starla's head felt clearer. She took a long gulp from her canteen.

I'm pathetic, she thought, back there I was going crazy.

She pressed the points on the inside of her arm. Still nothing. She examined the skin. The red welts had gone. Perhaps she wasn't sick.

She leant forward, carefully undid her boots, and pulled them from her feet. Where the blisters had burst, dark blood had dried around her toes. Angry pink sores formed around the places where her boots rubbed. She stretched out the toes, peeling them apart. Through her shirt, she scratched at the side of her abdomen.

She felt filthy. She wanted to wash. She wanted to eat properly. She hated the bread, it hurt her stomach, and she wasn't touching the jerky. She took another long sip from her canteen.

Ari stirred. She looked over at Starla.

Starla finished the water in her canteen and screwed the lid back on.

"Empty?" asked Ari.

Starla nodded.

Ari looked away. "Well, that's that then."

"What do you mean?"

"Well, all we got left is what's in my canteen. We're almost out."

Starla raised her eyebrows. "What?"

"No more water," said Ari.

"Where can we get more?"

Ari smiled. "The sky." She looked at Starla.

"But does it look like it ever rains 'ere?"

"What do we do?"

"Well, we're probably gonna die 'ere. Ya drank the water quicker than ya shoulda'."

Starla looked intently at the empty canteen in her hands. Where once it was heavy, it was now almost weightless. Water was life. A cage without a bird, like the broken ribcage discarded by the tracks; without life all you had was an empty shell. The difference between full and empty is the weight of existence. Starla looked at her scrawny arm; she'd not eaten properly in days. Soon she'd be as scrawny as Ari, and for the first time, she realised how much her face stung. Gingerly, she felt the dry, stiff skin.

I must be sunburnt, she thought. Just one more indignity. Well, don't just feel sorry for yourself, if you die out here it'll be because you let it happen. You, Starla Corinth. You are your father's daughter. You can do better than this.

She looked at Ari. "We're not going to die out here."

"What makes ya say that sister? No water, an' the big fella on our tail. I'd say we're pretty close to bein' outa options."

"But you don't know that. Maybe no one's following us. Maybe they'll carry on down the tracks."

Ari sucked at the corner of her lip. "Maybe."

But I'm my father's daughter. Corinths don't give in and die under a rock. Ari's losing faith but I won't. That skeleton on the tracks, that's not me. "We need a plan."

"Ya got one?"

Starla studied her canteen again. "We need water, we need supplies. If we walk now, in the open sun, without water we'll die. If people are following us, then it stands to reason they have water. So, why don't we take theirs? Why don't we fight?"

Ari grinned. "Because that'd be crazy. Ya not thinkin' straight. Best thing we can do is push on an' hope we find water."

"And where are we going to find water out here?"

"Ya forgettin' sister, I don't even need water. I still have some left in my canteen, that'd do me two or three days at least. I can go this alone. But you, ya dyin' out 'ere. Ya only gonna slow me down."

"You're forgetting our deal. You want in to the city then you get me there, and I can't spend another day walking right now. I'm out of water, my feet are blistered, I have to stay."

"I ain't forgettin' nothin'. But right now, what's the use of keepin' to our deal if I'm just gonna die out 'ere? Livin's livin' but dyin's dyin'."

"Fine, go then. But, the way I see it, out here living's not so different to dying. The way I see it, you've given yourself a choice."

"Yeah," said Ari, sitting up. "Well maybe I 'ave an' I think I just made it." She stood and, slipping her canteen over her shoulder, she stepped into the open sun. "Ya comin' Dog?"

The dog whined and rolled up next to Starla. She reached over and stroked its belly. "Looks like he's made his choice."

"Well fine if ya wanna play pets under ya rock." Ari slung the bag over her shoulder. "But I'll be seein' ya."

Ari turned and clambered over a nearby rock, leaving behind a stubborn silence.

CHAPTER 11

"Well, what do you want Max?" Starla paced across the room then turned to him.

With his left hand, Max massaged the back of his neck. Behind him, through the windows, morning light drowned the coloured lights of the city, bathing the spindle-like structures in a warm, yellow glow.

"I came to wish you a happy birthday."

Starla almost smiled but caught herself. "Well, thank you."

"It's not every day you turn eighteen."

"Well, I don't feel any different today."

"You want to watch it though, too many birthdays can be the death of you." Max grinned. Starla rolled her eyes. "I take it you'll be at the party tonight?"

"It's not like I can miss it."

"You don't want to go?"

Starla turned to the window. A monorail

train, working its way between the buildings, glinted in the sunlight. "Why should I want to go? Why should I want to go anywhere my father wants me to go?"

"But you'll be there?"

Starla's eyes narrowed. She looked at Max. His busy fingers toyed with the edge of his jacket.

"What's it to you?"

"Nothing," replied Max. "I was just making conversation."

"My father sent you."

"No one sent me. Look, I'm just here to wish you a happy birthday, that's all."

"Well, you've wished it me. I'll see you later at the party."

Once Max had left, Starla turned back to the window. It was unusual to see Max at this time. It was unusual to see anyone. There had been something strange about him. He almost seemed nervous. She remembered her father's words, only two nights ago:

"It's not about my legacy or yours, the succession of power is vital to our very way of life. With this, we secure all our future's."

△△△

Ari squatted in a crevice, a short way from where Starla lay under a rock. She studied the ground intently. She no longer had a plan.

She'd a mostly full canteen, plus food and supplies. She could still make the city, but she'd be stuck on the wrong side of the wall. She could make it back to Cooper, if that's what she wanted, she didn't have the dog but she could chance it with the dingoes. Or, she could go back for Starla.

The big fella, she thought. Ain't no crossing the big fella. What was Starla doing, dragging me out here with the big fella on our tail? How could I be so stupid?

A lump began to form in Ari's throat.

I could hand Starla over, but then what good would that do me? I'd be alive, but I'd be back on the salt plains, if they didn't send me to the ore mines just for getting mixed up in this.

Or I could go back for Starla…

If we run, how far would we get? Not far enough I reckon. I shoulda brought more water. That's my fault, if she dies out here Ari, that's on you.

And what if Starla's right…

But that's crazy talk, likely to get us both killed, two of them against men with weapons and Maker knows what else.

Then again, maybe we're not being followed? Maybe it's just us out here, and if so, we don't have enough water for both of us to make it all the way to the swamp. But, maybe we'll find water over the next rock?

And there was the hope, rising up and niggling at Ari's soul.

Give up now, and you give up on both Starla and the city.

Ari sucked at the corner of her lip.

The mayor's daughter. What do I owe her anyway? What do I care if she dies out here?

But Ari, you could make it to the city.

She reached inside her pocket and pulled out the lashes Starla had given her when they first met; two neat little crescent moons with perfect, bristly hairs.

What good do these do me? I've been starving, digging up salt with my bare hands, barely enough to eat, while people in the city were wearing these? While Starla was wearing these?

Ari closed her fingers into a fist, ready to crush the lashes.

All these years, digging in the salt, while people were wearing these.

Her blunt nails pressed into her palm and she felt the delicate lashes compress.

Why did I bring these and not the piece of glazed white porcelain with the part of the blue bird?

She thought of her little cave; the oil lamp, the bits of broken pottery and beads, the sketch on the wall; a little hut with the chimney and the two stick figures.

I should have scrubbed that out long ago.

She thought of the salt plains, hauling heavy buckets up the hill to the quartermaster.

One more mark against my name, what's it

gonna be worth today Ari?

Her shoulders and the back of her neck still ached where she'd carried the metal yoke. With her left hand, she felt the little indent at the base of the back of her neck, smooth and angular where the yoke bit.

How many buckets of salt did I haul up that hill? I shouldn't have even been there. I should have been in the city.

Ari thought of her bedroom in the city. Wrapped up in the darkness, between clean sheets, she'd watched the coloured lights twinkle along the spines of buildings.

Ari exhaled slowly. The heat in her gut began to subside. She opened her palm and, with her forefinger, she separated the two black lashes. As the light caught them, they released the slightest hint of blue.

Blue like Starla's eyes.

Long ago, Ari had the vaguest memory of her mother once wearing something like these. She remembered the sweet, perfumed smell of her mother's dressing table. She remembered drawing shapes in the spilled purple powder on the table top.

How many days had passed since then?

More than Ari could ever count.

Ari lifted one of the lashes between her thumb and forefinger and held it to the light. It was so delicate, like it might easily crush between her calloused fingertips, and so light she might not be holding anything at all.

Could I ever wear something like these? In some other life, somewhere in the city?

The idea was almost impossible, but only almost. To live the life she remembered, all those years ago. To live a life like Starla's. A life where she could want things, just because. Like the beads. Like the porcelain. Like the lashes.

The life she deserved.

So Starla might be saved. Water might be found. The city might still be entered. The salt plains could be forgotten, along with the hunger and the thirst and the absence of any kind of future.

She could have her future back.

But there was still the danger. What good was all this hope if she was dead? Going up against whoever was following them was just plain stupid. Ari didn't owe Starla her life. Ari didn't owe her anything. But she'd dragged Starla out here and abandoned her in the wasteland. That was her doing and her failure.

The lump grew in Ari's throat. She closed her fingers over the lashes and kicked the gravel with her boot.

"Dag it," she said aloud.

Dag it all.

Then the air was broken by the crack of a gunshot.

△△△

Starla closed her eyes and her mind drifted in and out of consciousness. She listened to the warm breeze drift around the rocks. The dog snuggled up against her thigh.

He should have a name, she thought. A dog needs a name.

Now Ari was gone, the dog allowed her to evade any nagging feelings of loneliness. She would sleep, then come up with a plan. All was not lost. She had shade and she was her father's daughter. So far, as they always had, events had worked themselves out. Sleep was what she needed now. Rest and recuperation. And anyway, Ari would probably be back soon. Let her go off and sulk somewhere. The girl probably needed a little time out. Perhaps they both did. Somewhere, at the edge of consciousness, Starla thought she heard a low, warbling sound, rhythmic and lulling her to sleep.

Starla awakened to the sharp, agitated sound of the dog barking. Her heart froze.

What am I doing, alone in the middle of the desert?

Her hands began to shiver.

She clambered out from under the rock. Her head spun and her throat was dry. Her heart thumped erratically beneath the thin wall of her chest. The dog, perched on the top of a large, smooth boulder, stood alert, barking into the emptiness.

What does he see? Are there dingoes?

She pulled on her boots. Against the stiff leather, her blisters stung, and she balled her toes. She slung the empty canteen over her shoulder. The dog kept barking.

She cried, "What is it dog?"

Crackkk.

Starla's heart jumped.

The sound of the gunshot echoed around the rocks. She looked back up the rock face.

The dog fell silent. Like a puppet whose strings had just been severed, its body crumpled. Leaving an angry red smear, its limp form slipped down the rock and came to rest in the dust.

Starla froze.

Three figures emerged over the rocks and began their descent. Starla recognised the bright red armbands. A scrawny young man brandished a large gun. The man with the milky eye. The other two, stocky and neckless, carried sticks like truncheons. The open sun reflected on their round, polished scalps. They looked like twins.

The man with the milky eye raised his gun. "Ya won't give us no trouble now. Ya not gettin' away this time."

Starla started to shiver. She looked about, searching for some kind of escape. The boulders rose up on all sides. She had no weapons. She tried to move but her legs felt like lead. Her eyes fell back on the lifeless dog. She raised her hands.

CHAPTER 12

Gingerly, Ari peered over the top of the boulder. Red armbands. The big fella's men.

If they don't kill you Ari, they'll send you to the ore mines.

Ari pushed the thought from her mind.

The party were making their way back towards the railway tracks. Starla stumbled with her head down, hands bound behind her back. A man walked behind, his gun raised. Every now and then, Starla would slip and one of the stocky men who walked beside her would grab her and pull her back up. Ari couldn't see the dog.

Keeping low and careful to stay out of sight, she followed them across the rocks. All the while, she considered what to do next.

It's my fault Starla was captured. I shouldn't have left her under that rock. She was my responsibility. And if she's anyones hostage, she's mine. My way into the city. But what am I gonna do about it? I'm out numbered and out gunned. But I can get ahead of them at least.

Nimbly, she moved from rock to rock. By late afternoon, as she slipped back down onto the railway tracks, by her own approximation she was well ahead of the party.

She followed the tracks a short way back until she came to a battered, dusty vehicle. It looked ancient. Its open body, raised high off the ground on four chunky tyres, was covered in welts of red rust. Behind the wheels, long grooves cut into the red dust. Ari placed down her bag and climbed onto the vehicle.

Inside were four canvas seats, and a large bay at the back covered by a hinged steel plate with a padlock. Taking her fire-starter and blade, Ari broke open the lock. She lifted the lid.

Inside, two red jerry cans sat side by side. Ari twisted open the cap of the first and a strong, metallic smell emerged. Fuel. Replacing the cap, she tried the second, it didn't smell of anything. She heaved it forwards and gently tipped it. Clear liquid splashed the canvas. Ari's heart leapt. Water. She twisted back the cap, heaved the jerry can over the side of the vehicle, and lowered it to the ground.

She found a bag full of some kind of dried meat and threw it over the side of the vehicle too. In the corner of the bay sat a small rucksack. Ari knelt and opened it. Inside, held together with a rubber band, she found a pack of dogeared playing cards. Stars, hearts, people in crowns. Ari had seen the big fella's men playing games with cards like these, but she didn't know how to play. There were shirts and bits of old rag. Ari felt around for anything useful like a knife and her fingers found a small, hard box that rattled in her hands. It was wooden and its scratched surfaces looked old. Ari lifted the hinged lid. Embedded under the lid was a mirror.

It had been a long time since Ari had seen her reflection.

A jagged crack separated the two sides of her face. She inspected her blotchy, tanned skin, baked hard and drawn around her eye sockets and cheekbones. Her teeth looked yellow, a large chip in her left incisor.

At the bottom of the box was printed a picture of a girl in a big, blue dress with long blonde hair, a silver crown on her head. Across it rolled several spent bullet casings.

Ari snapped the box shut.

Ain't got no use for a mirror anyway.

She stroked the fine bristles on the top of her head.

Ain't got no use for you either. It's too hot for hair.

Rising, Ari twisted open the cap of the other jerry can. She tipped it over and let the red liquid spill out over the interior of the vehicle. The strong, metallic smell stung her throat. She slipped back to the ground, re-shouldered her bag, and moved the water and meat behind a nearby rock.

Ari rooted inside her bag and pulled out Starla's dress. In the late afternoon light, the blue fabric shimmered. She tore away a strip of fabric. When she returned to the vehicle, an evaporating haze had formed above the spreading fuel. Ari doused the fabric in the fuel and retrieved her firestarter and flint. Two good strikes and the fabric burst into hot flames. She tossed the burning rag into the vehicle.

Yellow flames spread through the interior, licking around the seats and control instruments. Ari took a step back.

Then the vehicle exploded.

The force of the blast hurled Ari backwards.

△△△

Starla saw the plume of orange flame peal into the sky. The explosion rolled around the rocks like thunder. The man with the milky eye raised the gun to her head.

"Where's the other one?"

His one good eye bulged and his bottom lip started to tremble. His voice had a whine, like it had never properly broken.

"I told you," said Starla. "She left me."

"Where. Is. She?"

"How should I know? She left me. She didn't

care anymore. I told you, she's gone."

I'm not lying, thought Starla. She could be anywhere by now. I don't see why she'd stick around, not with these guys waving a gun around.

In the man's sickly thin fingers, the gun started to shudder. For just a moment, Starla wondered if he'd hit her with the gun barrel. There was something in the web of angry blood vessels around his iris, some restrained rage eager to escape. How long had he been holding onto his temper?

He lowered the gun barrel and kicked the ground. He looked at the other two men. "An' what're you two lookin' at?"

Like mirror images, the men looked at each other and shrugged.

"So what's your plan?" asked Starla. "To deliver me to the big fellow?"

"Well yeah, it just may be. An' ya can count yourself lucky an all. Ya don' really wanna be out 'ere on ya own."

Starla wasn't sure which option was better, to try to escape, or to accept the relative security of these men and whatever awaited her with the big fellow. At least they probably had water. She looked at the twins. Stocky and neckless, across their bare, leathery chests, black blotches spread like spilled tar. These men seemed scared to touch her. When she stumbled, they lifted her gently in their big hands, as if to straighten some delicate flower that had fallen in the wind. Despite their size, they didn't threaten her.

The man with the milky eye prodded her with the gun barrel. "So keep movin'."

△△△

Ari's ears rang, and the rotten smell of burning fuel irritated her nostrils. Dazed, a stinging pain flowed up her left arm. She dragged herself to her knees and inspected her arm. On the inside, from wrist to elbow, was a fresh, red burn. Though tender, the skin hadn't broken. It could have been worse. Ahead, thick black smoke spiralled upwards.

They won't have missed that, thought Ari. And they won't be going anywhere. Now they'll be on foot, and they've lost their supplies.

Ari got to her feet and brushed some of the red dust and black flecks from her clothes. She limped back and recovered the water and her bag. She heaved the bag over her shoulder, lifted the jerry can, and hauled herself back onto the rocks.

She ate some of the meat and topped up her canteen. Carefully, she bathed her burn in some of the precious water. On contact, the hardened skin stung. She would have to ignore it. Where she'd fallen, a large blue bruise had formed at the top of her leg.

The big red sun slipped over the horizon and the dingoes began their long, haunting song. Ari placed her hand on her blade.

I'm one of you now, she thought. I've no dog, no gun, but tonight I join you in the darkness.

As the darkness grew, she left her position, kept her body low, and worked her way back over the rocks. Finally, she spotted four figures moving slowly towards her.

Starla's probably tired, she thought. And she can't move easily with her hands bound. She's wearing them down and they're getting sloppy. But I'm not. I'm like a dingo.

Close by, from somewhere among the nearby rocks, a dingo moaned. Ari froze.

It's okay, she thought, tonight I'm one of you.

The figures had also stopped. Ari could just about make out muffled voices, but she couldn't hear the words. Then they moved on.

Ari smiled.

△△△

As darkness folded around them, and the dingoes began their chorus, the men pushed Starla on. At one point, a howl sounded close, and the men paused on the top of a rock. Starla squinted into the darkness, but couldn't see anything.

"Bloody dingoes," said the man with the milky eye.

We should have named the dog, thought Starla. He was a good dog, well behaved, and he was my friend. He deserved a name. And now there's no dog to keep away the dingoes.

She felt a sudden hatred for the man with the milky eye.

How could he take him away?

One of the twins spoke. "We should be careful boss. Maybe we should stop?"

"They're only dogs," said the man with the milky eye. "We don't stop till we're back at the truck."

Then, from right underneath them, moaned the distinctive call of a dingo.

CHAPTER 13

Ari hunched down underneath the rock and did her best impression of a dingo's call.

"Ahoooooooowhoo."

She stuck her head out, confident that in the darkness she was all but invisible. Right above her, the gunman swung his gun barrel into the darkness between the rocks.

Ari reached up, grabbed his ankle, and pulled him down into the crevice.

The man yelped. There was a crack as the gun went off. Briefly, both were illuminated by a hard red flame. One of the gunman's eyes looked bloodshot, the other milky white. Ari plunged her blade into the gunman's chest.

Then darkness. Ari's ears rang.

The man fell backwards and Ari came down on top of him. She twisted the blade. His hot body wriggled beneath her. She pulled out the blade and plunged it in again. Briefly, she felt it grate against bone. A shiver ran up her spine. Then the blade found a route between the ribs.

The body gurgled. Now, she could just make out its features in the moonlight. She withdrew the blade and grabbed the gun. She backed off from the body, allowing it to disappear into the darkness and out of her mind.

The two stocky figures were clambering down the sides of the rock. Starla was left alone. Ari scrambled up onto the rock and began to undo Starla's binds.

"Ari?"

"Shhh…"

She struggled with the knots, then used the sticky edge of her blade. Below, she could hear the men moving around the rock. One of them cried out. There were frantic scratching sounds, followed by a low growl.

"Bruce," called out one of the men.

"Dingoes," whispered Ari. "Where's the dog?"

"Dead. Are you hurt?"

"What?"

"The blood."

Ari shook her head. "It ain't mine."

Below, an anguished cry that barely sounded human was cut short.

An animal yelped.

On the other side of the rock, one of the men scrambled up and Ari met him with the gun barrel.

"They got Bruce," he said.

Ari began to compress the trigger.

The moonlight caught the man's eyes and they looked like those of a child. Ari hesitated. The man let go of his stick and raised his hands. The stick slid off the rock into the darkness.

"They got Bruce," he repeated.

Ari read his thoughts as if they were her own. He was lost and alone in a vast and unforgiving desert. Out here, there was no one to save him. So he did what he could to survive, played the cards he'd been dealt. Perhaps he wasn't a bad man. Perhaps she wasn't a bad woman. Ari took her sticky finger from the trigger.

This ain't my blood.

From between the rocks, a huge dog pounced and sank its teeth into the man's torso. He didn't even cry out as he was dragged down into the darkness.

△△△

"Okay, what now?" asked Starla.

Ari and Starla stood in darkness on the top of the rock. They could hear the dingoes prowling below. Ari knew it was just a matter of time.

"I dunno."

"Thanks, by the way," said Starla.

"For what?"

"Coming back."

"Well, for now ya can save it. We ain't out of this yet."

Gingerly, Ari explored the gun. She'd never held one before. It wasn't as heavy as she'd thought. She'd seen the big fella's men carry them, as they patrolled along the edge of the salt plains. From down on the salt, the guns had always looked heavy and cumbersome. Now in her hands, it seemed light and agile. She wondered how many more shots it had. Maybe there were more bullets with the gunman's body? Or back at the vehicle? Not that either would do her much good now.

I guess there wasn't much point in burning the vehicle.

Below, the whining had stopped. The world had fallen strangely still.

Starla whispered, "Maybe they've gone?"

Ari shook her head. "They ain't gone nowhere." They'd got the scent now, and no dog to deter them. It was crazy that a little mutt like that could ward off these monsters. Well, thought Ari, the big fella's men came all the way out here with this gun. This thing better mean business.

A large, dark, shape crawled up the side of the rock. Ari froze.

Don't scream Starla, she thought. Please don't move or make a sound.

Its red eyes glinted in the moonlight. A body larger than a man's, shoulder blades oscillating between ripples of muscle. The creature sniffed the air, steam blew from its big nostrils. Ari's finger trembled against the trigger. The animal snarled and bared incisors like white daggers. Ari levelled the barrel with the animal and squeezed.

The trigger was heavier than she'd expected, until the final moment when it slipped home suddenly. With a crack, the weapon ricocheted upwards and Ari was thrown backwards.

The creature pounced and landed on top of her.

The dry fur smelt dank and oily. Ari wriggled beneath the heavy animal. Claws tore at her shirt. Its breath smelt metallic like blood. She pressed the barrel of the gun into the creatures belly and fired.

The animal lurched and, from somewhere deep in its gut, escaped a low whine.

Ari heaved the heavy body sideways. It slid off the rock.

Ari tried to catch her breath.

Starla looked down. "Are you…"

"I… I'm good." Her heart pounded at such a pace it hurt. She rubbed her eyes. Floating in the centre of her vision, she could still see the flash of the gun. Carefully, she got to her feet. "Okay, now move." Ari leapt onto the top of the next rock and stumbled. She held out her arms, steadying her feet, then turned back at Starla. She hadn't moved. "Now!"

Starla looked about herself but didn't jump.

"Sister, ya gotta move."

"What about the other dingoes?"

"We gotta chance it, ain't no stayin' 'ere."

Starla leapt and landed with a wobble beside

her.

Ari nodded. "Okay, now we keep goin'"

Ari leapt to the next rock, then the next. She heard Starla scramble behind. Ari heard more yelps and howls below, but didn't stay long enough to explore them.

Ari made it to the tracks first. Standing by the rail, Starla stumbled down after her. She fell on the ground at Ari's feet and grabbed hold of her leg.

"You came back."

"Strewth, I told ya to save it." She kicked her away and Starla sat on her knees and began to weep.

A huge creature slipped out from between the rocks. Ari raised the gun to it and tensed her shoulder muscles, ready for the upwards movement of the gun when it fired. She took a step forward and the animal stopped.

It panted, mouth open, tongue lolling between ugly canines. In the moonlight, its eyes flickered like hot coals.

Ari took another step forward and the animal retracted.

Nothing attracts dingoes like a dead dingo, thought Ari. But they don't like other dogs, and tonight I'm the dingo. This is my world now.

Ari raised the gun and fired into the air. The crack echoed out around the rocks. The animal whimpered, turned tail, and leapt back among the rocks.

Ari exhaled slowly and smiled.

"The dingoes. They don't like loud noises."

CHAPTER 14

Ari recovered the supplies and they spent the night huddled against the railway tracks. Ari stayed watch, cross-legged and wrapped in salt sacks. She leant against the upright gun and gently shivered. Beside her, Starla slept fitfully. She cried out at one point, perhaps from a dream. She reached out and took Ari's hand.

Ari flinched.

Starla's hand gripped tighter. It was soft and warm.

It had been a long time since she'd touched anyone, except the gunman. His body had felt warm too.

Ari shuddered.

She remembered driving the blade into the man's ribcage, and the way it had grated against the bone.

A shiver ran down her spine.

She'd never killed anyone before. It was easier than she'd thought. Alive, dead, was it so different? Someone is there and then they're not.

It had to be done. It was him or me.

She remembered her mother.

People die, that's what they do. Everyone does, they live and they die and they go back to the earth. And I had no choice, it was him or me. We're safe now. That was because of me. Dingo or man, it's all the same. Ain't no difference at all.

She could no longer feel her heart beating, as if an icy hand had reached inside her ribcage and stopped it dead. Now there was only her and the land and Starla and the dingoes and the body among the rocks, but nothing more. The world was smaller now.

Gently, she squeezed Starla's hand.

She remembered the warmth of the body. The sticky blood on her hands.

She released Starla's hand.

And she was alone.

△△△

High in his tower, Titus Corinth stood at a large window and surveyed the luminous, ever shifting vista of the city. Monorail trains moved on strings of neon across a sea of blinking lights and between great chasms of steel and glass. The mayor held his hands behind his back, his fingers tightly interlaced. Intermittently with his thumb, he squeezed the fatty lump at the base of his small finger.

"Where was the last contact?"

The voice that answered, muffled in static, came from speakers hidden throughout the room. "Cooper."

She was lost in the wasteland. The town of Cooper had been searched and searched again, though nothing was easy on the outside. The town was a waste overflow of desperate people. People who wanted to hurt the city. And people they needed. He tensed his fingers. And there was blood in the abandoned van, but it wasn't Starla's.

The mayor pursed his lips.

The disembodied voice spoke again. "And what about the girl?"

And, thought the mayor, what about the girl. This girl, whoever she was, was now someone with purpose. People lied to themselves, they thought they needed shelter, food, security, love even. But none of this was true, and when the hour came they'd sacrifice it all for purpose. Purpose is what each and every person really needed. Only then were they truly alive. And now this girl had purpose.

She might prove useful yet.

Unexpectedly, the mayor thought of Starla's mother. His eyes moved to the inky blackness beyond the wall. He hadn't thought of her in a long time, not since she'd been cast out from the city, along with her lover and that bastard child. He couldn't have hidden them any longer. He hadn't even wanted to.

She's out there too, he thought. Somewhere in the wasteland…

Elsewhere in the city, Max Panache charged down a long, dark corridor.

If you want something doing, he thought, do it yourself.

At the end of the corridor, a wide doorway lead out onto a landing platform perched on the side of the steel tower. A large, black aircraft waited, squat with dipped wings, each embedded with a round propeller. The propellers spun and the engines hummed. A hatch on the side of the aircraft lay open. A guard in a light blue uniform stood on either side of the hatch, their faces hidden behind heavy visors.

The outside. Max clenched his fists as his father's words echoed in his mind. "You are a disappointment my boy."

Well, I'll show him. Before this is over, he'll eat his words.

Max got to the top of the ramp. He paused, then turned to look at the two guardsman. "Tell me Gentleman, have you both had breakfast?"

The two guards looked at each other.

"Most important meal of the day, Gentleman. You can't kill anyone on an empty stomach."

CHAPTER 15

"But we're not supposed to come here."

"It's fine," replied Max, striding ahead. The freshly cleared land stretched outwards, hard and red, all the way to the new line of the wall. Starla squinted into the middle distance, towards the large cranes that moved steel plates into place. On the ends of robotic arms, welding arks sparked orange and blue as new guard towers were swung into place.

Earlier, Starla and Max had slipped away from their minders. There'd been no school that day. Starla wasn't sure why she'd followed Max. Max had been taunting her.

"Come on," he'd said, his big eyes glowing. "That is, unless you're chicken?"

"Shut up Max," she'd replied.

"Cuc-cuc-cuck." Max folded his arms and flapped them, bobbing his head forward and back.

Starla looked away. She squinted as the sun

caught the glass of the tall buildings on the other side of the lake.

"If we go now, they won't see us." Max nodded towards the two guards who sat dozing against a rock in the sun.

Max started backing away. He flapped his arms and grinned.

Starla rolled her eyes.

The newly reclaimed land was dry and cracked, and nothing like the grassy grounds around the lake. Behind them, the old wall was being dismantled one large section at a time. In this moment, Starla and Max were further than they'd ever been from home, walking on ground that only recently had formed a part of the world of the outside.

"Do you think this ground is safe?" said Starla.

"Of course it's safe. If it was contaminated, they wouldn't take down the old wall."

Something on the ground caught Starla's eye. It was small, metallic and half-moon shaped. She bent down and picked it up. She rubbed the surface with her fingers. Faintly, some sort of shape had been stamped into it which looked like a star. Starla almost called out to show it to Max, but then thought better of it. He'd probably take it and not give it back. Instead, she pocketed it.

Max was well ahead now and she called after him. "Wait up."

Max stopped and turned to her. "I'm not waiting for you."

Then he took a step forward and disappeared into the ground.

ΔΔΔ

"So what's the city like now?" asked Ari, walking a little ahead.

They followed the railway as it cut a wide curve through the red rock. A warm breeze clawing at the dry dust.

Starla wheezed. "What do you mean?"

Though her head was still dizzy and there was a dull ache at the back of her skull, today Starla felt stronger. After she'd woken, Starla had had her fill of water and, after much hesitation, she'd tried a little of the jerky. It had made her teeth hurt and now they felt loose in her gums, but at least she wasn't quite as hungry. I'm sorry, she'd thought, as she'd chewed at the tiny piece of meat. She'd thought of the dog and the animals in the city zoo. But I must survive this.

It was with a heavy heart that she now thought of the dog. She missed his stocky little body trotting by her heels. All morning, his absence played on her mind. Occasionally, she'd thought she heard him scamper in the dust, or she'd thought she felt his warm, fuzzy body press against her leg. Each time, she'd look down and see nothing but her ill-fitting boots and the red dust.

"The city. Alice," Ari continued. "I ain't been

there in so long."

"Well, it's the city. It's very different from life outside the wall."

"Different how?"

What does she want me to say, thought Starla? "Well, the food is better. And there's more of it."

With the thought of trays full of syntho cubes, her stomach rolled and her mouth began to salivate. She tried to push the images from her mind.

"And no one's trying to kill you. There's that too."

"Sounds good to me," said Ari.

"I guess. For me, it was just where I lived. I used to dream of the world beyond the wall."

"Really? That don' seem like much of a thing to dream about."

"I guess."

"Kinda strange really, now ya think about it, if you were dreamin' of the world outside the wall, and everyone else was dreamin' of life inside it."

"But this isn't how I pictured it," said Starla. "There's nothing here. This place is empty. It's like all there is here is us and the dingoes."

"Yeah, an' they ain't 'ere for the dust." Ari turned and looked at Starla. "They're 'ere for us."

"I just think, no wonder the people who built this railway deserted it. This place is dead."

Ari turned back to the horizon. "Yeah, well that's why everyone wants in to the city."

"I never really liked the city," said Starla. "I mean, it's home. Now all I want to do is get back. But I always felt kind of trapped there."

"What d'ya mean?"

"I don't know. Everyone was always trying to please me, just to get close to my family. Everyone except the Panache family. They wanted to control me. So did my father."

Starla thought of Max, her intended fiancé. It all felt so far away now, a part of another life. Maybe, she thought, I should marry Max. He might provide a certain security. Isn't that what the city does though? Isn't that why I want to go back? It can't be that secure though, or I wouldn't be here.

Then she thought of the old man licking his lips. She thought of the lifeless skull biting into the red dust. She thought of the angry red stain left by the dog. This was what life was, outside the city wall.

"I guess everyone in the city is scared," said Starla. "No one wants to leave. Exile is the ultimate punishment."

"Yeah," said Ari. "Well, I know that." She sighed. "Sounds like ya got some issues there sister. I tell ya what though, I've spent half my life diggin' up salt that goes to the city. There's ore mines too, that's what they make ya buildin's outta. An' opals. It all goes to Alice on the camels. How we supposed to build a city out 'ere when all the ore an' salt an' stuff goes to Alice? That's what I think though. Ya might have problems in Alice, but they ain't the problems ya have out 'ere."

Ahead, a pyramid-shaped hill reached upwards. They followed the tracks round, and behind the hill hid a massive metal machine the size of a building, all twisted and rusty pipes. Alongside the machine, the tracks forked. On one side sat a long row of large, rusty carts.

They followed the carts until they reached a stretch of tarmac road, potholed and cracked under the endless sun. Arranged beside the road lay a series of walled enclosures that might once have been buildings, along with a series of crooked metal poles. Starla wondered if, long ago, this might have been a town. Perhaps someone's attempt to build a city of their own? But, like the rest of the world, it now appeared abandoned and lifeless. A world baked hard under an endless sun.

They left the tracks and followed the road. Among the remnants of ancient buildings, this new world seemed more silent than the open desert and the railway. A breeze whispered around remnants of walls and doorways. Bits of bent metal, their purpose long forgotten, burst like weeds from the red dust. Further back from the road, as if someone had collected them recently, sat a mound of plastic bottles and synthetic materials; perhaps the last remains of whoever may have called this desolate place home.

They walked on, leaving the ghosts of buildings behind, and after a while the tarmac disappeared beneath the red dust and all they had to follow was the long line of crooked metal poles, stretching ahead into the distance. Around them rose low, rocky hills.

And silence…

Then, not silence.

A heavy, clanging sound, quiet at first and then louder as they got closer. Clang, clang, clang-clang.

"What's that?" asked Starla.

"What's what?"

"The clanging?"

"Dunno."

They continued onwards, and around another hill they found a large, square, metal platform that looked like it might once have stood on stilts. Two of its legs had given way and now it stood at an angle, one side digging into the dust, the other suspended. A piece of its rusty panelling dangled down. It flapped intermittently in the wind.

Starla and Ari paused.

Starla lifted her canteen and took several deep gulps.

From under the platform, waving one bony hand, appeared the figure of a scrawny old man.

△△△

Starla froze. The old man kept moving towards them. Ari raised her gun.

The old man looked as ancient as the landscape from which he'd emerged. It was as if he'd crawled up out of the dirt; a ghostly apparition as old as the rest of this forgotten world. Caked in red dust, his wiry frame was insufficient to fill his tattered rags. The skin that hung from his bones was tanned and leathery and seemingly merged with these wrinkled rags. He reached out one shaking, bony hand; the fingers were long with knuckles like knots in an old rope. His mouth was a toothless grimace but his pale eyes looked kind and gentle.

"No closer," said Ari, but he didn't stop.

Before Starla could bring herself to move, the old man had placed his hand on her shoulder.

"Pees," he whispered. "Pees."

Starla tried to speak but couldn't. Something twisted in her gut. She'd no fear of this old man, and had the feeling if she blew hard enough, he might crumble back into the ground. Instead, she pitied him.

Ari put the gun barrel to the old man's head. "Get off old man."

"Pees," he said again. "Wata."

"Water?" asked Starla.

"Don't give 'im any," said Ari. "We ain't got spare."

Starla's gut twisted and she resisted the urge to slap Ari. They had water, why couldn't they share a little? Starla glanced at Ari, Ari's eyes simmered. Defiantly, she offered her canteen to the old man.

The old man grabbed it and fell to his knees. He tipped his head back, lifted the canteen to his parched lips, and began to gulp down the precious liquid.

Ari reached out and snatched the canteen, spilling a little of the water. "We ain't got spare," she repeated.

"Pees," said the old man, holding out his palms, his eyes wide.

Starla looked at Ari. "We've got some more."

Ari scrunched up her face. "Fine. It's on your head though, we ain't 'ere for this sister."

Ari passed the canteen back to the old man who clasped it and continued to drink. Finally, he stopped and handed the canteen back to Starla. There was still plenty left, as if his birdlike gulps had barely touched it.

"Than' ya," said the old man.

Starla slipped the canteen back over her shoulder. Ari glared at her and gently shook her head.

"You're welcome," said Starla. "What are you doing here?"

To Starla, the old man seemed kind and honest. He was weak and thirsty and now wore the sad grin that only comes from having lost all your teeth. His pale eyes smiled.

The old man shrugged. "Lif 'ere I does."

"In there?" asked Ari, pointing towards the collapsed platform.

The old man looked at her and nodded.

"What is this place?" asked Starla.

"Is ol', li' me," said the old man. "I's too ol' to go on. Stay 'ere now. He loo' after me."

"Who's he?"

The old man pointed at the metal platform. "Is someone else there?"

The old man shook his head. "Jus me. Me an' my shell." He smiled at her. "Fol' build 'im, lon' ago. Gone now they are. Town dead, all dead, 'cept me. An' I, well, fol' gone before I finds 'im. But I says 'ere now. Thoughts I's be dead by now, but Maka, he go' other plan I guess."

"Why did the town die?"

The old man shrugged. "Maka, he know, bu' Maka no' says. People go ba' to the earth, li' me soon."

Ari sighed. She reached in her bag, pulled out some of the dried meat, and threw it to him.

The old man nodded to her and smiled. "Than' ya."

"Whatever," said Ari. "Come on sister, we ain't got time for none of this."

The man didn't seem to take offence. He just smiled and nodded again at them, and so they left him there, knelt on the ground and smiling. Starla turned away, and when she looked back he was gone, as if, as she'd suspected he would, he'd crumbled back into the red dust.

CHAPTER 16

The black aircraft flew low, tracing the full length of the ancient road between the city and Cooper. It passed by long camel trains, animals all roped together, and donkeys and carts laden with salt and ore one way and grain and weapons and whatever else the city could trade the other. On the busy road people stopped to look up. It was rare to see an aircraft from the city.

Later, just outside Cooper, the aircraft reappeared and landed by an abandoned van. The rear doors lay open; its wheels were removed. Max Panache and two guards descended from the aircraft's belly and began to fan out.

Max paused. He sniffed the air. Cooper, the town was coming in down wind. It smelt worse than a dead kangaroo.

△△△

All afternoon, they followed the line of crooked metal poles until they ended abruptly in the middle of a desolate plain. On the horizon, a ridge of rocks and some dark shapes shimmered in the haze. Closer, the dark shapes formed a line of sparsely leaved gumtrees that reached jaggedly upwards.

At dusk they reached the tree line. They set up camp among the white barks and for the first time they built a fire. In the half-light, Ari disappeared off among the bare trees. Starla moved closer to the fire, soothed by the warm glow. When Ari returned, she presented Starla with what looked like small, knobbly lumps of wood.

"What's this?" asked Starla.

"That's a bush coconut."

Starla rolled it between her fingers. "What do you do with it?"

"Ya eat it."

Ari took back the fruit. Using her blade, she split it open to expose its milky white heart. In the middle was a fleshy bit of slime which Starla thought she saw move.

"What's that in the middle?"

"That'll be the grub," said Ari.

"The grub?"

"Ya know, baby insect. He lives in it."

Starla grimaced.

Ari smiled. "Ya wanna try 'im?"

Starla shook her head.

Ari winked. Between two fingers, she plucked up the gooey creature and popped it in her mouth. "He's good," she said, chewing. "Sweet."

As it grew darker, they moved closer to the fire, and somewhere, far away, the dingoes began to howl.

"We should be right tonight," said Ari. "We got a fire; we're in the trees. I reckon they won't come too near."

They slept between the trees and Starla once more dreamt of her father. In the dream, she was much younger. Her father sat at a long table in his office and looked down at her as she approached. Agrippa Panache sat opposite him.

"Where is Max?" she asked. "He wasn't at school."

Agrippa avoided her gaze.

Her father stroked his chin. "Max has been moved to another school. You won't see him anymore. Now run along my dear. You should be asleep."

"But where is he?" She knew it was important.

Her father grew stern. "My dear, you should be asleep. Now run along and don't worry about such things. We're very busy, we don't have time for this."

The room slid away. She was out in the corridor and the corridor was growing longer and longer with more and more doors on either side. She was running down it, trying the doors, but every one she tried was locked. Finally, she fell through one and found herself on the outer side of the city wall. She spun around, intending to turn back, but there was nothing but opaque wall. The doorway was gone. The wall towered above her and stretched out impenetrably on either side. Her heart began to race. She beat her fists against the wall, screaming as loudly as she could. "Let me back, let me back." She beat the wall until her fists hurt and all her energy was exhausted. Finally, she collapsed onto the dusty ground, leant against the wall, and clasped her head in her hands. Her body shivered and she could feel a cold sweat coming on. When she awakened, she was still shivering.

It was dark, the fire was now just a few cold embers, and briefly Starla thought she heard that same low warbling sound she'd heard back at the rocks. She strained her ears but the sound was gone. Looking up, she caught sight of Velle Stella, blinking between the branches. Then the shadows of the bare trees closed in and the world felt slightly less empty.

△△△

"But why can't I go there?" Starla had protested. "I want to go."

Starla got everything else she wanted so why not this?

She'd stood on tiptoe and clasped the railing,

her gaze affixed beyond the city wall. The barren wasteland stretched to the horizon, a place of infinite possibility and adventure.

Her father looked down at her and sighed. "My dear, why do you think we built the wall?"

Starla furrowed her brow. "I don't know."

"Come my dear, you must have some ideas."

"Because… I don't know. Because it's stupid."

Her father was being stubborn and she'd hated him for it. She'd angered when her teacher had evaded the same question. Why couldn't she visit the lands beyond the wall? Her classmates had looked on her with horror while her teachers had cowered. They always did when she confronted them. Other children were disciplined, but she was carefully dispatched home. After all, she was the mayor's daughter.

"What if I told you the wall was built for your protection?"

Starla tightened her grip on the railing. "Was it?"

"It was."

Starla examined the long line of steel balustrades and concrete ramparts, guard towers faced inwards. "So what are we being protected from?"

"Many things. For one, the people beyond the wall. Yes, there are contagions to consider, but beyond that, we've worked hard to build this city. Brick by brick and stone by stone, we built this city and everything in it and it belongs to us. But out there, beyond the wall, there are a lot of jealous people."

"Why can't they come here?"

"Because they don't want to come to the city, they want to take it from us. They cannot understand our way of life so they seek to destroy it. If they were to come here, they would destroy us."

Starla's eyes traced the spindle-like steel towers. They looked delicate against the wall and the vast world beyond. "So that's why we built the wall? To stop them destroying the city?"

"Yes."

Starla leant her chin against the railing. None of this really explained her first question.

"But why can't I visit the outside?"

"Because, my dear, nothing is as simple as all that. We must lead by example. You see, as much as we are protecting the city from those on the outside, we are also protecting it from those on the inside. The city doesn't just belong to us, we also belong to the city. It is our duty to stay. But sometimes, people in the city can forget how important the city is. They forget how hard our predecessors fought to build this place. This city was hard won. And this is where we belong now, working together, safeguarding this way of life from those that might take it from us. We should always remember that, and the wall is a useful reminder. We should not concern ourselves with the outside world. For us, all we see beyond the wall is foreign, it is not our concern. Out there, if they wanted to, those on the outside could build cities just like ours. But they choose not to, and that says plenty about why they do not belong here. So my dear, don't trouble yourself with what is beyond the wall. It is not your place. You belong here in the city. And one day, when you're older, you will realise you don't even want to visit the lands beyond the wall. One day, it will not even cross your mind to think of them."

"But what if I still want to visit them?"

Her father's eyes had narrowed. "Then my dear, there is always exile."

CHAPTER 17

With dawn, they moved on, deeper into the barren woodland. It seemed the further they went, the larger the trees.

"What is this place?" asked Starla.

"Old folks always called it the bush. We're gettin' closer to the swamp see. There's water near. That's why there's trees."

"Most of these trees look dead though."

The trunks were bleached a ghostly white, and only the smallest green leaves clung to their upper branches.

"Well, I think they's just pretendin'," said Ari. "In this country, nothin' wrong with playin' dead sometimes. Playin' dead could save ya life."

This whole land is playing dead, thought Starla. Whatever happened here, it happened long ago. This was a place the world had forgotten.

Back in the city, the glass-covered gardens were full of trees. Great trees, with rich brown trunks and large, green leaves. Around them grew plants with colourful and heavily fragranced flowers. Little birds and butterflies fluttered between the branches and everything was alive. These trees were not the trees of the city. This was the forest of the dead.

Sometime later, Starla thought she heard a rushing sound like that of running water. It filtered between the bare trunks, gradually growing in intensity. Then the landscape broke, falling away at their feet into a broad crescent-shaped valley. Below, fast moving water glittered in the sunlight, flanked by huge rocks and ghostly gumtrees. In the distance, a dense forest of vibrant green assaulted the landscape.

Starla looked down at the river, running fast and clear, and fought the compulsion to leap off the rocks and dive down beneath its fresh and cleansing waves.

"We go down there," said Ari, and pointed far below into the valley. "An' we follow the water almost all the way to Alice. At the end of the river is a dam an' then there's the city."

"So we're close?"

"Well, closer."

At the thought of heading towards the water, Starla inwardly grinned. Perhaps she could swim in the river and finally feel cool and clean?

Gingerly, they made their way down the face of the gorge. Deep shadows formed pools of alluring shade that were almost as enticing as the running water. A fresh breeze came up off the river and Starla found herself wondering why anyone would live anywhere else but here. It was truly beautiful. She'd seen no place closer to those she'd spied in the backgrounds of paintings in the city archives. Perhaps, she wondered, such places do exist.

Her boot slipped on a loose rock and Starla almost lost her footing. She stopped and watched the rocks tumble all the way to the frothy water at the bottom. Looking down, she felt dizzy.

"Careful," said Ari, going ahead. "Ya fall in, I ain't gettin' ya out."

Then the path gave way, and Ari with it.

Starla could only watch as Ari tumbled down towards the frothy depths.

△△△

Ari's lungs contracted. In the darkness, tumbling beneath the waves, she lost all sense of direction. Desperately she clawed, and the heavy water dragged through her fingers.

She struck a rock hard, then the water grabbed her and pulled her onwards. Her head broke the surface and she gasped, then the current pulled her under again.

Her heart thumped against her breastbone and a red heat rose in her gut.

I can't swim.

She thrashed her arms. Over and over she tumbled. Her hand broke the surface of the water and was washed down again.

I might die.

With her hands and feet, she searched for anything with which she could take hold. A sharp object scrapped painfully against her palm and was gone. Her head bobbed to the surface. A flash of colour, a mouthful of air and water, and she was dragged under again.

Darkness. She screamed into the water.

Her body thumped against something hard and round and, as she began to drag around it, she reached around and hugged it. Her head breached the surface and she gasped. Roaring, the frozen water dragged at her limbs. The surface of the rock was smooth and slippery and she clung tighter.

She was out in the middle of the river. The cold water stung her face; from below her chin, the rest of her body was going numb under the water.

Ari searched for Starla. The imposing rock face loomed above. The narrow shoreline looked far away. "Starla," she cried, her voice lost in the surging din.

Has she fallen too? Is she drowning somewhere further back or further down the river? Each way she looked, she saw only the chopping grey waves and further on a thin mist.

Water. First you've not enough, then you've got too much.

She tried to pull herself further up the rock but she only slipped further down. She leant her head back, keeping her mouth above the surface. She took in a mouthful of water and choked. Her jaw chattered, her limbs numb. Her joints were starting to burn and the water was ceaselessly pulling at her and she knew it wouldn't stop.

Oh please she prayed, Maker don't let me die here. Don't let this be it.

She couldn't feel her fingers.

Her hands slipped and she was pulled back under.

$$\triangle\triangle\triangle$$

Starla watched Ari disappear beneath the waves. Her skin started to tingle.

"Ari," she cried out to the water below.

She scanned the water down river and saw nothing but choppy grey waves in a thin mist.

She can't be gone, she can't be.

Ari, don't leave me.

Her hands started to tremble.

Down river, Starla saw Ari's head emerge. Ari looked like she was struggling, trying to stay afloat. Then she disappeared beneath the waves.

Starla knew it in an instant. Ari can't swim.

And the water's moving fast, she thought, I'll never make it down to the riverbank in time.

There was no other way. Time was running

out and if she was to act it had to be now.

Starla leapt off the side of the gorge.

△△△

Starla struck the water hard and instantly her bones ached. Pain bubbled up in her chest as if, briefly, the cold shock had stopped her heart. Then she was rising to the surface, slowly exhaling. Holding out her arms, her head bobbed above the water and her feet scraped the riverbed.

I'm lucky I didn't strike it when I landed, she thought.

The current took her quickly down river.

Starla remembered the rivers and lakes of the city. In the hottest summer months, the population flocked to their soft, cool waters and long, sandy beaches. This was nothing like that. This water clawed at Starla and tugged her along with it. It was all her efforts to keep her head above the surface and she let her body flow with the fast movement of the current.

Ahead, she saw Ari raise her head. Starla pulled at the water, trying to manoeuvre herself. It was easier to grab or kick rocks at the bottom than to fight the current.

Come on Ari, she told herself, grab hold of something. You have to stop moving else I'll never catch up.

She spat out a mouthful of water. The chill

hurt her gums.

"Ari," she cried out.

The water howled.

Ari, whatever you do, don't drown. Don't leave me here, lost and alone, but also, don't drown.

Finally, she spotted Ari on the surface. She was out in the middle of the river, clinging to a rock, and Starla was heading straight for her.

△△△

Starla struck the rock and gripped hold of its smooth surface. Her blue fingers had started to wrinkle. She dug her boots into the riverbed and battled the current.

Ari had her arms wrapped around the rock while her body was flowing away with the current. Her head was barely above the water and she was gasping and coughing. Not too much further on, the river was flowing over the edge of a waterfall.

"Ari," cried Starla over the din of the water. She put her arm under Ari's shoulders and tried to steady her. "Put your legs down."

Ari gasped desperately. "What?" she managed, choking on water.

"Your legs, put them down."

"I can't"

"You can. It's not deep."

Fighting the current, Ari managed to get her feet down and she pulled herself a little out of the water. "I can't swim."

"It's shallow, you don't have to."

"The current, it's too strong."

"Up ahead I think there's a weir."

"The fall. I told ya, I can't swim."

Starla squinted downriver. It didn't look high, or at least she didn't want it to look high. Really, she'd no idea. She looked back at Ari. "I think it's only shallow. We should make it to that and then climb over."

Ari's teeth were chattering. "I dunno."

"Well, are you going to stay here then? It's the only way and you know it."

Ari screwed up her face and nodded. "Okay."

"I'll take your hand. Then we let go."

With her wrinkled fingers, Ari gripped Starla's hand. She looked scared, her pale eyes wide.

Starla squeezed Ari's hand. "Let go of the rock."

Ari let go and they were moving fast with the current again.

Ari and Starla spun in the water, anchored by each other. Starla was pulled under and came up gasping but still she gripped Ari's hand. They struck a rocky ledge at the edge of the fall and the heavy water rolled over them.

Starla reached desperately over the ledge with her free hand and heaved herself up onto it. Once up, she pulled at Ari's hand and between them they both climbed up onto the ledge. Ahead, the fall wasn't too high.

Starla was closest to the shore; she started crawling along the ledge towards it. Ari followed. Coughing and spluttering and soaked through, they made it to a little dusty beach. Starla lay back on the grey sand and closed her eyes, listening to the rush of water beating passed them down the river. Ari collapsed next to her and, for a while, they both lay there, recovering and shivering.

Gradually, Starla's heart started to slow. She felt a sickness at the back of her throat. Her belly felt full of river water.

Then Ari sat and held her head between her hands. "We lost the supplies," she said. "An' the gun."

CHAPTER 18

Max Panache stood beside the opening of a small cave. He held a torn off scrap of blue velvet in one hand and a broken piece of glazed white pottery in the other.

The blue fabric caught the sunlight and glinted. Max rubbed his thumb against the fabric, feeling the thousands of tiny bristles. The pottery had blue markings on it that looked like part of a bird.

From out of the cave appeared a guard in a light blue uniform. He carried what looked like an empty hessian sack. On it was a small, dark stain.

Blood.

"Sir?" asked the guard.

Max Panache walked over to the guard. He looked down at the sack.

"Should we test it?"

Max shrugged. "I think you should knit your underwear with it, but let's try your idea."

For some time they sat on the beach and watched the water rush by. Finally, Starla broke the silence. "Is that it then?"

Ari shrugged. "Maybe." There was a slight shake in her voice.

We're screwed now, thought Ari. Ain't no point going on. And who does this girl think she is? Leaping in and saving me. I didn't need no saving. That's not how this works. I woulda been fine. I ain't never needed nobodies help before and I don't need hers now.

But doubt crept into her mind.

I was weak when I needed to be strong.

Starla spoke again. "Well, I've still got my canteen, and we've got plenty of water now." She nodded towards the river.

"Yeah, well maybe you should get us to Alice with ya canteen."

Starla raised her eyebrows. "Well you've still got your canteen too. What else have you got?"

Ari sighed and rolled her eyes. She didn't even know who this girl was now.

Seriously, does Starla even need my help? The way she's acting, she might as well just go off and find her own way to the city.

But to humour Starla, Ari reached in her pocket and pulled out her metal fire-starter and flint and a couple of bush coconuts. In the other were the two lashes; she quickly closed her fingers over them and put them back in her pocket. Strapped to her ankle, she still had her blade.

"Can you find more of those?" asked Starla, pointing at the bush coconuts.

"Sure. Ya can find 'em everywhere."

"So, we got food, we got water, we can make a fire. I reckon we can still do this."

Ari sucked at the corner of her lip. Starla was probably right, and that annoyed her even more.

I can't believe I let that happen, she thought. It's embarrassing it what it is. And how am I supposed to know how to swim? Ain't no place to swim in Cooper. Ain't no water like this anywhere but here. But here, you can't swim in the water because it's too fast and, for pretty obvious reasons, you can't swim down river. Not unless you want to be eaten. Out here, ain't no reason to learn to swim. Maybe the water didn't beat me and maybe Starla didn't beat me. Maybe I beat myself? And look at Starla now, all high and mighty and full of herself.

You coulda died out there Ari. Died like the man back at the rocks.

She pushed away the memory.

And what about the supplies. Was that my fault?

She remembered the way the blade scraped against the edge of each rib.

It don't matter either way now. The supplies were lost, somewhere down the river. Maybe they'll turn up, maybe they wouldn't. Maybe's no use though, maybe leads to hoping and then you're gonna fall. The gun's probably lost completely and just when we could use it most.

"Fine," said Ari. She got to her feet. "Come on then sister, you lead us to Alice."

But, before she gave Starla a chance, Ari walked on ahead along the edge of the river.

△△△

Head down, Ari walked ahead. Starla simmered.

Why was Ari so ungrateful? She hadn't jumped into the river so that Ari would thank her, but she deserved at least some acknowledgment.

But you need her, thought Starla. But do I? I jumped into the water and saved her.

But Ari is the one who knows the way. Without her, you're lost out here.

Starla called ahead to Ari, "Look, whatever your issue is right now, I'm sorry."

"It's fine," said Ari.

Well I'm pleased about that, thought Starla. She knew everything was not fine.

A little later Starla tried again. "Listen, whatever it is…"

Ari cut her off. "There's no issue right. It's fine."

They continued onwards in silence.

The valley opened up into a large crater full of white gumtrees, surrounded on all sides by a rocky shelf. The sun was setting and the air was growing cooler and the crater was almost entirely in shadow. They followed the river into a clearing where a rusty vehicle sat decaying under a tree.

"All right," said Ari. "We camp 'ere tonight." She walked off into the trees and Starla was glad of a break from Ari's sombre mood.

Starla explored the vehicle. It might have once been a car with a bench at the front and another at the back. Preceding the front bench was a thin wheel and a series of faded, rusty dials. The bench itself was a twisted mesh of rusty wire and exposed springs, but the rear bench still had a dusty plastic covering, heavily worn and almost white. There were no doors, only spaces like missing teeth where doors must have once been. The four wheels, one on each corner, had all but rotted away leaving only stumps behind so that the chassis sat on the ground. This was not a car that would be going anywhere far any time soon.

I wonder how this came to be here, abandoned and left to rot. I wonder who left it here. I wonder if they made it much further.

She shuddered and pushed the thought from her mind. She climbed through the empty doorway and into the back. It smelt musty but not unpleasant, like the back of an old wardrobe, and the springs, lumpy under their plastic covering, were not uncomfortable. It was nice to be under a roof again. She sat back, resting her head against the backrest, and closed her eyes.

When Starla awakened, it was almost dark and Ari was sitting by a gently crackling fire that spat embers into the night air. Starla climbed out of the car and sat down by the fire. Without looking at her, Ari passed her a stick with some kind of charred lizard skewered on it.

"Thank you," she said and Ari nodded in reply and went back to staring into the fire.

Starla ate quietly. The meat was sweet if chewy. Before this afternoon, she might have protested at such a meal, but now she accepted it without question. This was what there was and there was no use arguing. It was them or the lizard. If she wanted bush coconuts instead, she probably should have found them herself. That was how it was now. And she didn't want bush coconuts. The lizard was surprisingly edible. She washed it down with water from her canteen, which she'd topped up from the river. It was still ice cold.

Once she'd finished, she returned to the back seat. Moonlight glowed through the empty rear window behind the bench. It was comfortable here and strangely homely. It was being inside, under a roof. It seemed like a long time since she'd been anywhere that felt remotely homely. But here was a place made for and by people. A human burrow.

She leant back in her seat, ready to fall asleep, when Ari climbed into the seat next to her.

CHAPTER 19

Starla jumped.

In the darkness, Ari wriggled around in the seat for a few moments then was still.

"Kinda comfy," she said.

"Yes," said Starla.

"Look," said Ari. "Thanks for, ya know, in the river."

Now Starla felt petty for having ever wanted any kind of acknowledgement. It didn't matter at all as long as Ari was okay.

"That's okay," said Starla.

"Thing is, I ain't really used to havin' anyone lookin' out for me. I never needed no ones help before." She fell silent for a moment and averted her eyes from Starla's. "Thing is, I don't know how to swim."

"That's okay."

"It's not, I nearly drowned out there. It was stupid, goin' down that slope by the river. We didn' have to go that way but, I dunno, I thought it'd be quicker."

Starla reached out and took Ari's hand. It was warm and dry. For a second she thought she felt Ari flinch. "It's okay, really."

Ari looked up and her eyes caught the moonlight. "So where'd ya learn to swim anyway?"

"Years ago when I was little. We've got swimming pools in the city. And these huge lakes full of fresh water that you can swim in to cool off."

"Sounds crazy."

"There are rivers too, that run through the arboretum. The trees are a lot greener than these. You can swim in those too and the water is so warm it's like taking a bath."

Ari rested her head against the top of the backrest and stared upwards out of the rear window. The twinkling stars looked like tiny holes in a dark blanket.

"I don't remember ever havin' a bath."

"Not even in the city?"

"I was only little when we left," said Ari.

"Why did you leave?"

"Well…" Ari seemed to hesitate. "It was a long time ago an' it ain't a happy story."

"Not every story's happy."

"Well, this one sure ain't. See, it was all down to my folks. Ya probably know that back in the city, if city folk disagreed with anythin' then they gotta leave. First time I saw ya, I figured it were probably the same. An' once ya leave, there ain't no goin' back.

"Well, that was my folks. I don' even know what they disagreed with. We had this apartment. I remember it had blue walls an' purple doors an' these lights that shone up from the floor. An' we had this little floor with railin's that looked out over the city. At night there were so many lights, of every colour ya could think of. An' we ate the syntho cubes. I liked the yellow one. I don't even know what that tasted like now."

The corner of Starla's lip curled. "I like the yellow syntho."

"But that's it," said Ari. "What does syntho even taste like? It tastes like yellow or green or blue or whatever. But it all tastes good right. An' I had this dress, it was yellow too. But I hated the dress. I always wanted to dress like the boys. I don't know why. Anyways, that's what Alice is to me. It's never bein' hungry an' it's my folks bein' happy an' everythin' being fine. An' then one day my Mum wakes me in the night an' says we 'ave to leave. I don't know where I'm goin' or anythin' like that. They just say we 'ave to leave. They pack some of my things in a bag an' then we go outside an' there's a car waitin' for us with a friend of my Dad's. We drive to the city wall an' my Dad's friend leaves us there an' we carry on driving."

"What happened to your parents?"

"Ya want the whole story?"

"Sure."

Ari sighed. "Well, at first it's okay. We moved

into this hut out in the desert away from everyone. My Dad took the car out one day an' came back with this horse. He told me it was a pony an' I thought it was the best thing ever. He used the horse to go get supplies an' that's how we lived. We just kinda pretended we were still in the city. I actually found it all kinda exciting. I got to feed the horse an' learn to ride 'im an' my Mum got better at cookin' all these interestin' foods. I didn't like 'em at first but ya get used to 'em an' ya start to really like 'em when ya cook 'em right. My Dad built this whole other room on the side of the house for me. He build this chimney out a' rocks an' mud an' we could 'ave fires inside an' that was really great... But then my Mum got sick. She got so sick she couldn't get out a' bed. So my Dad said he was goin' into town to get medicine... an' he never comes back."

"What happened to him?"

Ari seemed to shake her head.

"Dunno. He left an' I never saw 'im or the horse again. For a while I thought he left us but now I reckon somethin' else happened. Like somethin' happened to 'im in town. Maybe be got robbed. Maybe he fell off the horse an' something happened. Guess I'll never know."

"I'm sorry."

"It's okay. Anyways, Mum just got sicker. I didn't know where to go for help or what to do. She was coughin' up blood and couldn' hardly breath. She looked so old an' her skin was pale an' yellow an' so cold to touch. Ya could see her bones through her arms. She couldn' eat nothin' then. One day she takes my hand an' I'm kneeling by her bed an' she says 'Ari, you have to leave me, this is the end for me.' Anyways, I weren't goin' nowhere. I stayed right there by her side, givin' her water. It was about all I could do anyways. Weren't no help to her otherwise, couldn' do nothin' else. But I wasn't goin' anywhere."

$$\triangle\triangle\triangle$$

Ari stared up, through the back window. Her eyes glazed over and she was far away, in another time, another place. Then they sharpened and she was looking far beyond the stars into the depths of space. She stared into the infinite emptiness found at the end of all things.

"Then one mornin', I woke up an' she was dead."

$$\triangle\triangle\triangle$$

Starla squeezed Ari's hand. "I'm sorry."

The moonlight caught the tears that trickled down Ari's cheeks. A lump formed in Starla's throat.

"It's okay," said Ari. "It's not ya fault. It's their fault. They left the city. They moved to some hut in the middle of the desert. They were stupid. They shoulda' been closer to town. Closer to fresh water."

"Still…"

"Still, whatever ya do people die. That's what they do. They live, they die. That's what everyone does. Don' take much. People are weak. Ya gotta be strong, ya gotta look after yourself. My folks were weak. It was their fault."

Ari fell silent.

"I'm so sorry," said Starla.

Ari exhaled slowly.

Starla said, "But you can't think that about your parents. That it was their fault."

Ari looked at Starla. "I can't? I can't?" She pulled her hand away. "Who are you to say that? You ain't never lived out 'ere. I 'ave. An' they were my folks. They shoulda' been there. They shoulda' looked after me. I should be in the city."

Ari's shoulders began to shudder and she dipped her head.

"Hey," said Starla, taking Ari's hand again. "I'm sorry, look, it's okay. I'm sorry. I shouldn't have said that."

"No, it ain't okay. I tried ya know. I tried to go back. I went to the wall an' they wouldn't let me in. They wouldn't let me in."

Ari's voice was breaking. Starla put her arm around Ari's shoulders.

"It was their fault. They were so stupid. An' I hated them for it for so long… An' I miss them…

I'm sorry"

"That's okay," said Starla. "I'm sorry too."

"I do miss 'em. Sometimes I dream about 'em. Sometimes I dream about our home in the city."

"Here," said Starla. With her thumb, she tried to wipe away the tears on Ari's cheeks. She remembered the evening in the cave, so long ago now it seemed, when Ari had done the same for her. "And you know, trust me, sometimes I hate my father too."

"Thanks," said Ari.

"That's okay."

"But seriously, out 'ere ya gotta be strong. Out 'ere ya just another wild animal tryin' to survive."

"You know," said Starla. "Sometimes, in the city, I felt like a zoo animal. Like the whole city is one big zoo, locked in behind the wall. I have my cage in the tower. And no one wants to leave the zoo now. We're like pet birds that have lost the will to leave their cages. Out here though, well I guess I'm free."

"Maybe," said Ari. "Maybe it's better in the cage though. At least they feed ya there."

"You know," said Starla, "I never knew my mother."

"What do ya mean?"

"Like, I never knew her. I've no memories of her. It's like she never existed. When I was younger I used to wonder where she was. I'd ask my father, he'd say she was gone. And that's it. So I stopped thinking about her. The city's strange like that. You just don't question things. You're told how things are and that's how they are. So I stopped asking, I stopped thinking."

"And now?"

"And now, I don't know. Maybe it's better this way. I've no bad memories of her. Nothing to resent of her. Maybe that's better?"

△△△

The black aircraft had landed in the darkness, somewhere near the rocks where the land was flat. Max Panache stayed close to the craft while two guards scrambled over the rocks, armed with guns and equipped with halogen lamps. They were gone some time.

Max paced back and forth impatiently, his hands clasped behind his back. He chewed the bottom of his lip and every now and then he gazed into the horrifying emptiness of the wasteland. Somewhere in the darkness, some kind of wild animal howled and Max shivered. The howl sounded almost human and like it was taunting him.

Starla could be anywhere.

Finally, he glanced upwards to the cold, hard stars. Indifferently, Velle Stella stared back.

What do you care, he thought? The star that never moves, goading the world below with one unblinking eye, while we all make fools of our-selves. But it never tells. It sees all and it never tells.

The problem with stars is that they're just too Sirius.

When the guards returned, they informed Max of the remnants of three bodies, partially eaten. None of them Starla's. Max didn't ask how they knew they weren't Starla's. The thought of partially eaten bodies was enough to turn his stomach. Evidently, food on the outside wasn't what it was in the city.

But there were tracks, footprints leading north, towards the city.

CHAPTER 20

Ari awakened, on the back seat of the car, to the shrill sound of a bird cackling happily on the bonnet.

The bird was stocky, with a round, grubby body, dark brown wings and a long pointed beak. It chortled rakishly towards the sky and was joined by a second that pranced proudly back and forth along the edge of the bonnet before turning to the first and returning a cackle.

Ari grinned.

"What are they?" asked Starla.

"They're guuguus. But some folks call 'em laughin' birds."

"They don't sound like they're laughing to me."

"They kinda do to me. Occasionally they'd visit the hut an' folk'd call 'em guuguus but then they'd say they were laughin' birds."

Ari climbed out of the car and stepped towards the birds. They didn't fly away, but kept on calling to her. She slipped her hand to her ankle and drew the blade.

"No don't," said Starla, drawing to Ari's side. "They seem like friends."

"They are," replied Ari. "Land gives ya what ya need." The birds were their friends; they were here to help them.

"I don't want to eat them," said Starla.

"Sure ya do."

"I don't and I won't. Ari, don't kill them."

Dag it.

Ari lowered the blade and looked at Starla. Starla's wide eyes glistened and her forehead crumpled. Ari looked away and a lump bubbled up in her chest and rolled up her throat.

Starla likes the birds, thought Ari. She likes the birds like she liked the dog. Well I like the birds too, but the world gives you what you need but not always when you need it. You take what you can. You take the bird, you eat it, it returns to the earth to be reborn.

And out here it's kill or be killed.

"Please," said Starla.

Ari sighed. She waved the blade at the birds. "Go on then, be off with ya."

The birds cackled and leapt into the air and flew away.

"Thank you," said Starla.

"Yeah, whatever."

Ari avoided Starla's gaze and slipped the

blade back in the sheath on her ankle.

Wasting two perfectly good birds, she thought. Could have had one easy. It was there for the taking, I could have just reached out and grabbed it. Why was I listening to Starla all of a sudden?

But when she'd looked in Starla's eyes she'd felt awful.

Why did I suddenly care what this girl thought? I should have taken one of the birds, she thought.

"We gotta make progress," said Ari. "And I'm gonna 'ave to find us breakfast."

△△△

They followed the course of the river, out of the crater and through a narrow gap in the rocks barely wide enough to squeeze through. The walls were cold and wet and they were deafened by the sound of rushing water. On the other side, the boulders were smooth and slippery. Finally, the ravine opened up into a broad valley that rolled gently downward. Hardy green and purple grasses clung to the rocks. Ahead, away from the river, was a dense green forest. As they got closer, Starla became aware of an intense, high pitched chatter. At first it sounded like hundreds of children, all babbling at the same time.

"What is that?" she asked.

"What's what?"

"The noise."

"Bats. Thousands of 'em."

They left the riverbank and headed for the trees. All the time the chatter grew louder.

They entered a forest of tall palm trees, solid and branchless at the bottom but bursting at the top with great green leaves. Beneath the cool, dark shade of the forest canopy, the sweetly acidic stench was suffocating.

Starla's eyes begin to water.

Above, the upper palms were heavily laden with large black shapes. She wiped away the tears with her palm. It took a moment for her eyes to adjust to the dim light, and then she saw them moving among the palms.

"Are they dangerous?" asked Starla.

"Sometimes they'll bite ya. Depends how hungry they are. But we're safer here than by the river."

"What's by the river?"

"Crocs."

Better the bats then, thought Starla.

She squinted up at them. From down on the ground, they didn't look so large. With their little furry bodies and wings they wore like dinner jackets, their chatter was almost welcoming, and their party was one she might want to attend. And in that moment, Starla decided she liked it in the forest.

The deeper they went, the more beautiful

Starla found everything. The great columns of palm trees formed the foundation for the lush green canopy. The effect was like some grand cathedral, sprouted up from the desert floor.

Slick with sweat, she tasted the acrid air, and her head started to spin.

Maybe I could stay here, she thought. I could build a house among the trees. I wouldn't have to go back to the city. Maybe I should bring Max here? Or maybe not Max, maybe I should just ask Ari to stay.

She looked about, at the tree trunks and the lush evergreen above, and the deep shadows in dark corners that beckoned her to curl up and sleep among them, and she felt love for everything. What was the smell and the chatter of the bats; they were nothing compared to the beauty of this place. Here was a place she could truly call home.

A colourful butterfly landed on her arm and she stopped and inspected it. It had four vivid, aqua blue wings with black tips. It tiptoed lightly on her skin and Starla knew she'd made a friend. It was inviting her to stay and Starla wanted to accept.

Yes Mister Butterfly, I would very much like to accept your gracious invitation. Nothing would give me greater pleasure than to stay here forever.

And she knew that nothing else mattered now she'd found this place.

And look, even the butterfly's wings were blue.

Her head felt dizzy. The butterfly flew away and she sat down on the ground and closed her eyes. The world spun around her. The guano smelt rich and sweet. Then Ari was leaning over her, shaking her.

Why am I lying on the ground?

"Hey, stay with me sister."

Ari's eyes are very pretty, she thought. Not in a conventional way, but in an Ari way. But why are they so cold?

△△△

Starla awakened to a dull pain in her head and the sound of water lapping against a riverbank. Ari leant over her and dabbed her forehead with a damp cloth. Her eyes were darting back and forth warily and drops of sweat dripped from the bristles of her shaved head.

"What happened?" asked Starla.

"Ya lost it. It's the bat shit, it sends ya loopy. I shoulda thought."

Ari raised the canteen to Starla's mouth and she took a couple of gulps and spluttered.

"Ya gotta drink," said Ari. "We can't stay 'ere. It's dangerous. We gotta get back in the trees." She glanced back at the river again.

"Okay," said Starla. She tried to raise herself

on her elbow but her head was too dizzy. Her vision blurred and her whole body seemed to vibrate. She felt Ari's arm, steadying her.

"We gota move," said Ari. "Water's too still, we shouldn' be 'ere."

Then a huge gaped mouth, lined with a serration of jagged white teeth, emerged from the water and clamped down on Starla's leg.

CHAPTER 21

Starla screamed as the huge green crocodile bit into the lower calf of her right leg. The animal grunted and stared at them through two green, slitted eyes, perched at the back of a long, thickly armoured snout.

Ari gripped Starla around her shoulders and tried to pull her back but the animal pulled them both closer to the water and Ari fell to the ground.

The animal hissed.

Ari drew back her foot and kicked as hard as she could. She struck the animals snout.

The animal twisted its grip on Starla's leg and Starla cried out again.

Ari struck again and this time her foot met the point just above the jaw, between the animals flared nostrils. The crocodile let go just long enough for Ari to pull Starla away.

The massive creature leapt from the water.

Ari got to her feet and began dragging Starla,

by her shoulders, into the trees.

The armoured monster advanced, dragging its fat belly over the narrow beach and waving its tail.

Ari heaved Starla over her shoulder. Starla wasn't heavy; her body felt thin and bony. Ari stumbled into the trees, her knees buckling with the added weight on her shoulders.

Behind them, the crocodile hissed and grunted. It ventured just into the tree line but came no further.

Why, thought Ari, was I so stupid to return to the river?

Her heart pounded. She stumbled through the trees with an energy she didn't realise she had. Her whole body pulsed. She tripped over vines and slipped on big green leaves. Then the ground disappeared and she was submerged in a pool of hot water.

Starla's body rolled above her. Ari tried to push her away.

The water felt thick and heavy. Ari's foot kicked against something hard.

Ari's head breached the surface and she gasped for air. Steam rose from the water forming a think mist. Frantically, Ari reached out for the edge and her hands grasped a vine.

Ari dragged herself out of the hot water. On her hands and knees, she choked. Water gurgled up her throat and she thought she was going to vomit. She heard Starla's plea.

"Help."

Starla was clasping hold of the rocky ledge at the edge of the water.

Getting to her feet, Ari moved quickly around the pool. Leaning, she gripped Starla's shoulder and pulled her over the ledge. Starla dragged her wounded leg behind her.

Ari wheezed. Her eyes stung and she rubbed them with her knuckle. Then she inspected Starla's wound. A bloody half-moon crescent was carved from the top to the bottom of Starla's left calf. The teeth had torn deep and it looked like there were chunks of flesh missing. It wept a thin, watery blood that leached into the forest floor. At least she still had her foot, for now.

Starla whimpered quietly. "Is it bad?"

△△△

"We need to stop the bleedin'," said Ari.

Starla lay on her front, right cheek to the dusty floor. Her left calf throbbed and a strange tingling ran from her knee down to her toes.

Ari undid her shirt. Under, she wore a grubby vest. Ari soaked the shirt in the warm water of the spring. "This ain't gonna be perfect," she said. "But we gota stop the bleedin'."

Starla could hear Ari tearing at the shirt, pulling apart the seams. Ari wrapped part of the shirt around her calf, then she pulled it tight and

Starla inhaled sharply. The fabric stung against the wound.

Ari slumped down breathless next to Starla. "Ya gotta stick with me sister. Ya gota stay awake. Think ya can walk?"

Starla wasn't sure. Her calf throbbed angrily. Pushing herself up on her elbow, she tried to stand and a hot pain shot up her leg. "I don't know."

"Well, we ain't got a choice." Ari slipped an arm around Starla's shoulders and lifted her. "Come on." She heaved Starla up on her feet.

Starla wailed. A solid pain shot up her leg. Even bending the ankle hurt. She collapsed against Ari.

"We gotta do this," said Ari.

"I can't." Her head spun and her vision blurred. Painful shockwaves bounced up and down her body.

"Hold on," said Ari, placing Starla's arm around her shoulder.

"Please, I can't." The pain seemed to be getting deeper, moving into her bones.

"Listen sister," said Ari. "I dragged ya this far an' ya ain't quittin' on me now. If we stay 'ere we're done for. The bat shit'll make us crazy an' if ya stay down 'ere bleedin' the bats'll get ya. So before nightfall, we gotta be outta 'ere an' that's that, okay."

CHAPTER 22

At dusk, the sky filled with a great dark cloud of bats. They chattered and squeaked and flew as one towards the desert.

Maybe, thought Ari, the bats won't smell the blood? They won't come too near the fire anyway, if I can keep it going. She pushed another dry twig between the glowing embers.

Now Starla slept. Ari had made camp just outside the forest, where Starla had collapsed. In the growing darkness, she'd gathered as many leaves and other forest debris as she could and covered over Starla's wound. Starla had barely made it, her left leg was useless and Ari had had to drag her all the way.

Why, Ari thought, was I so stupid? Where the river currents slowed, there were always crocs. I knew that. We shouldn't have stopped there. This whole area is croc country. You'd be safe if you were at least a croc's body length from the water.

Those were the rules. I knew that. So why did I carry Starla there? This is on my head now. I let this happen. I should have warned Starla.

Ari tipped a little water onto her fingers.

And why didn't you warn her Ari? Why'd you go putting her in danger? Because you thought you knew it all didn't you. You thought, how dare this girl go coming into your life and saving you from the river. That's not how it's supposed to be. Well, it's how it was wasn't it Ari.

Ari washed Starla's face and moistened her lips.

This is all your fault Ari. And now what you gonna do? How long till Starla can walk again?

The surrounding hills disappeared completely and night set in. Ari drew closer to the fire. All night, she added wood to the fire and checked on Starla. When dawn broke, Starla's eyes flickered and she murmured.

"Water."

Ari put the canteen to her lips and Starla swallowed a little and spluttered.

"Ya had me worried back there."

Ari cleared away the debris from Starla's leg. The fabric had dried hard to the surface of the wound.

It don't look any better, thought Ari.

"How does it look?" asked Starla.

"It's okay," Ari lied. "Ya gotta rest up though."

"I can do that."

Starla closed her eyes and seemed to fall

asleep.

Ari sucked at the corner of her lip.

What you gonna do now Ari? I could leave her. Just walk away and let her fend for herself.

But she'd thought this before, back in the crevice in the rocks. She hadn't left her then and she knew she wouldn't leave her now.

Well you gotta do something Ari. If nothing else, we need supplies.

She ventured to the riverbank and filled her canteen. The current was slow and Ari watched the dark waters warily.

If you're gonna get me, you're gonna get me. I probably deserve it anyway.

Ari explored a wide circle around the portion of valley she found herself in. She collected a number of bush coconuts she found growing on the branches of gumtrees. She was lucky enough to find a blue tongued lizard, sunning itself on a rock. They were dozy animals; it didn't move when Ari approached it, and it barely seemed to flinch when she slipped her blade into its back. She also ventured back into the forest and collected some large green leaves and some dried palms.

Back at camp, Ari arranged some of the big leaves on the ground. She shook Starla awake.

"Ya can't stay on the dirt, sister."

Starla was slick with sweat and her skin was clammy and red; she was lying out in the hot sun.

Dag it, I shouldn't have left her here. She'll be burning up.

Ari shuffled Starla gently onto the leaves. She raised her canteen to Starla's lips, and once she'd swallowed a little, Ari took her blade and split open one of the bush coconuts.

"Eat this," she said. "Ya gotta eat."

Starla swallowed a little and grimaced. Ari pushed more of the white flesh towards her mouth but Starla shook her head, her lips tightly shut. Then she closed her eyes again.

Ari busied herself with the dried palms. She dragged over a hunk of dead gumtree and arranged a canopy over Starla's head and the upper part of her body.

Starla's left leg looked really bad. Ari emptied the canteen's remaining water over the wound. Starla didn't stir and Ari wondered if she could feel it now. Gently, a layer at a time, she tried to peel away the fabric, but it was dried solid over the wound.

I could cut it away, she thought. But she didn't dare do so. Finally, she abandoned her treatment and arranged the palms over both legs. That should protect Starla from the sun at least, and hopefully the bats.

Ari refilled both canteens at the river and retreated back to camp. At dusk, the bats once more filled the sky; a vast aerial procession pouring from the forest and into the coming night.

Ari built a fire and roasted the lizard. Starla slept soundly. Ari ate most of the lizard. She had to keep her strength up, she would be no good to Starla otherwise. The rest of the meat she wrapped in leaves.

She sat in the dust by the fire and watched it spit orange embers up towards the stars. Ari hadn't slept in two days and her eyes were heavy.

Come on then, she thought, dingoes and crocodiles and bats and even people, if you're gonna get me then bring it on. Tonight's your chance.

She hauled the biggest log she could onto the fire and then she lay down in the dust and closed her eyes.

△△△

Ari awakened with a start. It was dawn and the light was thin and orange. Starla was breathing shallow and fast.

Ari went to Starla's side. Starla's clammy skin was greyer than before. Her eyes were closed. Ari took Starla's shoulders and gently shook her.

"Starla, wake up."

Starla didn't respond. Ari felt Starla's forehead and drew away quickly. She was burning up.

Dag it, thought Ari. Starla, you can't have a fever now. Please, not now.

She tried to give Starla some water but it just trickled down her cheeks. Ari put down the canteen and buried her face in her hands. When she lowered her hands they were wet with tears. She sniffed and wiped her eyes with the inside of her palm.

Dag it Starla, not this. Not the sickness, not the fever.

Ari had seen this before. She'd seen it in her mother. First you got the fever, then you died.

Come on Ari, she told herself, pull yourself together. Starla ain't your mother.

But still, she looked into Starla's face and instead she saw her mother's.

But I can't save you Mum. I couldn't save you then and I can't save you now. I can't do anything. I'm useless. We should have been closer to town, she thought. I should have been closer to town. That way we could get medicines. We could get the powders and the potions. But I couldn't because I was too far from town.

"Dag it," she said aloud.

I was too far from town. And now I'm too far from town again.

Ari got up and ran from the camp. Several yards away she collapsed on her knees. Her body was shivering. She was so tired, so weary. It was like her limbs were weighted with stones. All her life she'd run from this. She remembered the day her mother died. That fateful morning she was so still and cold. Her eyes were open and they stared blankly at the dark ceiling. She'd tried to close the lids but they wouldn't close. Her skin was so thin; so cold and yellow and stretched tight over her skull.

Ari remembered covering her with a thick blanket, the sort that itched to sleep under. She'd left her there, lying under the blanket. Then she'd packed a bag with what she could carry and she'd left the hut forever.

Ari dug her hands into the ground and lifted up handfuls of the powdery red dust. It trickled through her fingers like blood. And here she was, alone, far out in the swamp. And Starla was dying.

△△△

The black aircraft skimmed across the wasteland, kicking up a storm of red dust. It left the railway and the remains of a lost town. It headed east through a low valley and came to rest next to an ancient, collapsed canopy that was once a filling station. A wizened old man came out from under the canopy, shielding his face from the swirls of dust, and hobbled towards the aircraft. The engines wound down and then were silent. A hatch on the side of the aircraft opened and two guards descended. Max Panache followed them. The two guards approached the old man. Briefly, they spoke with him, then one raised his gun while the other returned to Max.

"Anything?"

"He's just a crazy old man," said the guard.

"I can see that. Search the platform."

The guard scampered over to the collapsed

canopy while Max wandered over to the old man who now knelt on the ground with his hands raised. The old man peered with pale, anxious eyes at the gun. The fear made him look younger somehow. His bright, wide eyes were those of a child's.

"Two girls find themselves lost in the waste-land," began Max.

The old man's eyes widened.

"They come across a lamp. They pick up the lamp and rub it, and out pops a genie. He tells the girls they may each have one wish. The first girl, well, she says she wants to be home, back in the city. The genie says of course, flicks his fingers, and the girl is gone. But what does the other girl say?"

The old man shook his head.

"This other girl, she's from the outside, and she says, 'Well, it's awfully lonely out here, I wish I had my friend back.'"

The old man's bottom lip began to quiver.

Max looked either way, then back at the old man. "Have you seen anyone come through here recently?"

The old man's fingers started to shiver.

"A girl from the city, and someone else? An outsider. Perhaps someone from Cooper?"

The old man shook his head. "Is jus' me an' 'im 'ere."

"Who else, who's here?"

"Jus' me, 'im look afer' me see."

The other guard was returning.

"Well?" asked Max.

"Empty, no one else here."

There was a trail leading from the platform but the footprints were starting to fade into the red dust. All around the platform were the bare footprints of the old man. They formed maddening spirals in the dust.

Max returned his gaze to the old man. "Now, I'm going to ask again. And nicely, because I'm a nice guy. At least two people came through this valley. I think you saw them. So tell me, what did you see?"

The old man shook his head. "Jus' 'im an' me 'ere"

Max leant closer. "Who, old man, are you talking about?"

"Jus' me."

Max stood upright and began to pace in circles around the old man.

"Am I not asking politely? Am I not being good to you? Is there anything at all unreasonable in my request?"

The old man just shook his head.

Max stopped pacing and leant closer to the old man again.

"Am I speaking English to you?"

The old man shook his head, his face long, mouth drawn open revealing a single grey tooth.

Max kicked the old man in the gut and the old man keeled over. His skeletal frame came to rest on its side in a foetal position, knees bent inwards.

"Look old man. Just tell me what I need to know."

The old man whimpered quietly, holding his gut.

Max began pacing around the old man again. "Come on old man, I don't have all day. I've things to do."

The old man rasped for air. "I's ol' see, they's hel' me."

Max stopped pacing and bent over the old man.

"You know, I'm not sure I understand a word you're saying."

"Hel' ol' man."

"What?" Max cupped his hand to his ear. "Speak up old man."

"Maka kee's me'."

Max stood upright and kicked the old man hard. His foot met the base of the old man's back. There was so little of him, Max wandered that his foot hadn't gone right through the old man's spine. He raised his foot and kicked again, his foot striking a boney shoulder. Pacing around, he kicked the old man again, this time in the belly. The old man's body deflated like air leaving a balloon.

When Max stopped, the old man's body lay still.

Max caught his breath, his heart racing. His fingers shook with sudden violent excitement. He looked between the old man and the collapsed canopy. Then he turned to the guards.

"So, who's for lunch?"

CHAPTER 23

All day, Starla never woke. She just lay under her shelter, her head in the shade, her breathing rapid, erratic and shallow.

It was at dusk, just after the bats had flown overhead, as Ari sat glumly by the fire, that she first noticed the drone. It rolled along the valley walls for short, intermittent bursts. Ari remembered hearing the sound before. She'd been alone in the wasteland, on her way to Cooper, her mother lying dead under a blanket. The bag she carried was heavy and she'd resorted to dragging it through the dry dust. She'd rested a moment, and then she'd heard the low, warbling sound.

Googa-goo-ga-ga-googa-goo-ga-ga

Just as then, the hairs along her spine began to rise.

She listened now. She couldn't tell how far it was away, sometimes it sounded close, others it was far off.

Googla-goo-ga-ga-goolga-goo-ga-ga

Perhaps the wind was catching it, but there was no wind in the valley. Ari felt the outline of her blade in its sheath by her ankle.

Ari added more wood to the fire then checked on Starla and tried to give her more water. She seemed to swallow a little but she didn't wake. The rest trickled down her cheeks. Starla looked thinner than she'd done yesterday. The fever was working fast, wearing her away. Her bones were drawing through her skin, like formerly buried alien shapes emerging from the dust.

That night, Ari slept further from the fire. It was cooler, however, she reasoned, if someone were to investigate the fire then here she would have the opportunity to startle them. She slept with her hand resting on her ankle, and she dreamt of her mother. In her dream, she awakened to find her mother dead, her mouth gapped open, her eyes gazing upwards. Her grey skin was drawn in over her skull, the cheekbones and eye sockets hollowed out. As Ari had stood over her, her mother had grabbed her wrist with skeletal fingers and Ari woke startled, clutching her blade.

Dawn approached, and the last cold embers glowed in the dead fire. Ari shivered. She could still feel her mother's cold fingers on her wrist. From a distance, the drone warbled. The pitch fluctuated, and then it was almost speaking to her.

Darlia-dead-dead-Darlia-dead-dead.

It fell silent.

Stiffly, Ari crawled across to Starla. She still lay unconscious. Her breathing was erratic. Ari wiped Starla's face and moistened her lips with a little water, then Starla's eyes flicked open.

Ari's heart leapt. Starla's eyes were dark, like black holes in hollow eye sockets. The deep blue was almost drained from them, and the pupils were heavily dilated. Starla moved her lips.

"What is it?" Ari asked.

Starla's lips moved again, but no sound came from them.

Ari leant closer. "You need somethin'?"

She just heard Starla's faint whisper. "Leave me."

Ari sat up. "I ain't goin' anywhere."

Starla stared back. Then she closed her eyes.

Ari shook her. "Stay with me."

But Starla was unconscious again.

Ari sat back and wiped her face. Her fingers were damp. She felt utterly helpless. She could do no more. But she wasn't going anywhere. She was back at her mother's bedside, waiting for the inevitable. She remembered the last time her mother had looked at her. Her eyes were so pale and lifeless, the pupils only pinpricks in a drained grey iris. And then she remembered the one good eye of the milky-eyed man, bloodshot, as she drove her blade between his ribs. She remembered the life leaving him. She remembered the darkness folding over him. She shuddered.

A life for a life, that's what it was. Sometimes

one life comes at the cost of another. I had no other choice.

She looked down at Starla. A life for a life. But Starla's ain't mine to give.

Ari spent the day foraging for supplies but kept returning to the camp to check on Starla. There was no change in her condition and she didn't wake again. Ari started to consider what to do when Starla died. Did she turn around and go back to Cooper and the salt plains or go on to the city? They were now well over halfway. But what good was going to the city if you couldn't get inside? You were never farther from the city than when you were standing right beside it, staring up at those opaque walls. You were no further inside than if you were a hundred miles away in the desert.

Again and again, Ari returned to Starla's bedside. Sitting in the dust, Ari closed her eyes and placed her palms on her eye lids.

Please Maker, she prayed, let this be quick and soon. I ain't never asked for much. I take care of my own, I don't need no ones help. But I'm not asking this for me, I'm asking it for Starla. Ain't no sense dragging this out. If she's gonna die let it be now and be done with it. Let her return to the earth and be reborn.

Ari removed the blade from its sheath at her ankle. She imagined sliding it across Starla's neck. She could make it quick, Starla wouldn't feel a thing. Just like finishing a lame dog or a horse. No sense prolonging the inevitable.

If you're gonna do it, she told herself, do it now and let it be done. Out here you've gotta be strong. Maker give me strength now. Let me help Starla one last time.

She remembered driving the blade between the ribs of the milky-eyed man and she shuddered. And she couldn't do it, not to Starla. Her hand shivered, then she let go of the blade. She was weak and had failed this final test.

I shoulda drowned in the river.

She felt wretched. She collapsed her face into her hands. When she finally looked up again, two tall figures, their skin so tanned it was almost black, were standing a short distance from the camp.

△△△

Ari recovered the blade and got to her feet. The two men stood stationary, looking at her. Ari knew who they must be. They were the Angu; the tribesmen of the bush.

This was trouble. Tribesmen could only ever be trouble. They carried a bad reputation in Cooper. There were stories of people who'd wandered into the bush and never come back. Stories of cannibalism and human sacrifice. There were a few Angu people in Cooper, working the salt plains, but they kept to themselves.

Thick, black beards covered most of their faces, and both wore the ragged, well-worn clothes of the outsider. One carried a long spear which he held upright. The other wore a wide brimmed bush hat, a satchel over one shoulder, but otherwise he seemed unarmed. From a cord around his neck hung a round, grey pendant, curved inwards like a small dish.

The man with the satchel stepped forward.

Ari raised the blade. "Don' come any closer."

"She's hurt," said the man.

"Yeah, so?"

"She need medicine."

Ari glanced at Starla then back at the man. "What's it to ya?"

The man raised his hands. He had kind, sad eyes, that held no anger. "She'll die."

"She's dead already I reckon. So ya just keep ya hands off 'er right."

"We can help."

The man took another step forward and Ari lunged with her blade. The other man leapt forward and levelled his spear. He grimaced and Ari almost dropped her blade. Her hands were shaking.

"Please," said the man with the satchel. "Medicine."

Ari's voice shook. "We don' need ya kinda help."

"Please," he said again. "We mean ya no harm."

Carefully, he reached inside his satchel and pulled out a wad of crushed green leaves and little purple flowers. He looked at Ari and gave her a broad, toothy grin. His eyes widened and he raised his eyebrows. He dropped down onto his knees next to Starla.

Ari kept her blade trained on the man with the satchel; the other man kept his spear trained on Ari. The man with the satchel had seemed to decide to ignore the standoff. He pressed his fingers against Starla's neck and sighed, shaking his head slightly. Then he inspected her leg and sighed again.

"What do ya want?" asked Ari.

"Jus' to help ya," said the man kneeling next to Starla.

He reached into his satchel and pulled out a bladder full of liquid. Ari watched him intently as he soaked Starla's leg thoroughly. Carefully, he began to peel away the material Ari had used as a bandage. Underneath, the wound oozed with a yellow pus. He lifted the leg a little and soaked the wound again, washing away some of the pus. Then he took the green leaves and purple petals and pressed them into the wound. He took from his satchel some bigger green leaves and he wrapped these around the leg. Once he was finished, he stood and met Ari's eyes again.

"We'll be back later," he said. "Don' go doin' nothing crazy while we're gone. Ya friend needs rest."

The other man nodded at Ari, lowered his spear, and backed away. Ari watched the men turn and disappear back into the bush. Briefly, she kept her blade trained on their path, her hand still shaking, then she relaxed her muscles and lowered the blade.

Ari knelt back down next to Starla. Her colour looked no better, but her dressing was changed and this was something.

Ari looked back in the direction the men had come. Why were they helping Starla? If they even were helping Starla. She thought of the man's kind, sad eyes. There had been no menace in those eyes, only a slight sense of pity. And the tone of his voice was soft. And the other man could have taken her with the spear if he'd wanted to. Ari couldn't pretend in that moment she'd have been able to stop him. But he hadn't, instead he'd nodded and backed off. Now Ari didn't know what to think, and instead a weariness came over her. She lay down in the dust next to Starla and closed her eyes.

△△△

At dusk both men returned, this time they carried two long poles wrapped in canvas. Ari stood and drew her blade.

"Please," said the man with the satchel as he approached ahead. "Come with us."

Ari looked down at Starla, then back at the men. Could she stop them if she wanted to?

"Ya 'ere to help?"

The man with the satchel nodded.

"Why?"

He held his arm out towards Starla. "She needs more medicine, please."

She watched as the men unrolled the material between the two poles. Gently, they lifted Starla and placed her between the poles.

Maybe the stories in Cooper weren't true? Or maybe there were other tribes out here? Different tribes to those found on the plains. And besides, thought Ari wearily, at this point what does either of us really have to lose? No one else out here is offering to help Starla.

"Come," said the man with the satchel, beckoning to Ari. "Don' stay 'ere. Bad 'ere. Will die 'ere."

CHAPTER 24

The men walked ahead, carrying Starla, while Ari hung behind and followed warily at a distance. They gently climbed, working their way through thick grass that grew up to Ari's waist.

I never needed no ones help before, she thought. I was fine, I took care of my own. All until the river.

She watched the tall figures sway back and forth. The man with the satchel had taken the rear. She watched the shape of his wide brimmed hat.

Why are these men really here, she wondered? I am a stranger in this land; treat strangers kindly, for you never know when you might be one yourself. That don't mean I can trust them though. Nobody helps no one for nothing. And these are still tribesmen. Maybe they're helping now, but later...

Finally, Ari called ahead. "So what do they call ya anyway?"

The man with the satchel glanced behind and the pendant that hung from his neck caught the moonlight and blinked. "They call me Jirra. He's Koora."

It grew darker but the men didn't seem to need the light. Several times Ari stumbled in the long grass. After a short while the moon came out, big and white, and Ari could see better.

The party worked their way out of the valley, away from the river and over the crest into the bush. Eventually, they came upon a collection of dark, oval huts. At the round doorway of one of these huts, a curtain was drawn to reveal a room lit by the orange glow of an open fire. The men took Starla inside. Ari hung back but Jirra waited for her. When she didn't come forward, the man beckoned.

"Come, be with ya friend."

Ari hesitated. She looked about at the squat, bulky shapes of other huts, just visible in the moonlight. A chill whipped across the bush and Ari shivered. Inside the hut, she saw the welcome glow of the fire. She could stay outside and freeze or take her chances in the hut.

Inside, the hut was warm and had the sweet, burnt smell of wood smoke. The walls, formed from tree bark and mud, were supported between curved wooden ribs that met in the roof. Starla's bed was arranged in the centre. Next to it sat various small, clay pots. What looked like blankets were piled up in a corner, next to a small, wooden cabinet with dozens of tiny drawers. A faded pattern covered the drawers, it was almost invisible but it reminded Ari of the porcelain with the part of the blue bird. In it, she almost thought she saw the shape of another bird.

To one side was a stone fireplace with a chimney worked into the roof, not dissimilar to the one Ari's father had built. In the hearth, a small fire crackled.

Jirra knelt and undid the dressing on Starla's leg. He removed the leaves and flower petals from the wound that were now sticky with yellow pus. Then he stood and left the hut. A few moments later, a big old woman with a round face clambered into the hut. She knelt down next to Starla and inspected the open wound. Jirra followed her and seemed to be waiting in earnest for her verdict.

In her large hands, she took one of the clay pots. She removed the lid and tipped a handful of live maggots into her palm. When she seemed satisfied with the number, she sprinkled the yellow creatures liberally inside the wound. Then she took some fresh leaves and flower petals and packed them back into the wound with the wriggling maggots. She bound the dressing in fresh leaves. She turned back to Jirra, nodded, then heaved herself from the floor.

Jirra went to the cabinet and opened one of the tiny drawers. He removed something, returned, and knelt next to Starla.

"Take a seat," he said to Ari, indicating to the space by Starla's bed.

Ari sat.

Jirra moved to the fire and placed on the hearth two clay cups. He filled them with the dry, green leaves, and added water from the bladder that hung by the fire.

"These are for ya," he said. "You drink one, when ya friend wakes, she drinks one." He looked at Ari as if checking she understood.

Ari nodded. "Okay."

"Good. Now, stay 'ere, look after ya friend."

He stood, pulled the curtain aside, and left the hut, rearranging the curtain behind him.

They were alone. Ari looked at Starla. She slept, but in the warmth of the fire Ari imagined she already looked better. Ari picked up one of the clay cups; it was warm from the fire. She raised the cup to her nose, and the fresh, aromatic scent surprised her. She drew away and inspected the steam that curled off the liquid, then smelt it again. She took a sip; it tasted sharp but not unpleasant.

She leant up against the wall of the hut and fell into a deep, dreamless sleep.

△△△

Ari awakened with a start; the first pale glow of morning seeped through the curtain that covered the doorway. The fire had died to a few embers.

When she looked across at Starla, her eyes were open.

"You're awake," said Ari. She took the cup of lukewarm liquid from in front of the fire. "Ya should drink."

Starla raised her head. Ari moved the cup to Starla's lips and she drank a little.

"Thanks," whispered Starla. "Where are we?"

"The Angu helped us. Dunno why, 'ere 'ave some more." She put the cup to Starla's lips again. "They patched ya up right though. Dunno what they want but didn' 'ave much choice back there. Thought ya were a gonna."

Starla took two more gulps. Ari removed the cup again.

"Ya gotta get better before we can go on," Ari continued. "And we gotta make a plan."

But Starla closed her eyes and seemed to fall back to sleep.

Yeah, we need to make a plan, thought Ari. First, we need to know if we're guests or prisoners. My thinking is it could be either.

Ari looked about the hut. How long had it been since she'd slept under a roof like this? A proper one, with walls and a door and a fireplace. Not since her mother had died. She wondered that she'd fallen asleep so fast, in the calm indoor world of the hut, with its unfamiliar household provisions. She had the feeling of being home again, in a way she hadn't done in a long time. Her life on the salt plains had been a restless one; a period during which she'd felt constantly in transit. But here, in the hut, this must be the feeling she'd have every day in the city.

Ari looked back at Starla.

I didn't leave her then. Should I have done?

Gently, Starla's chest rose and fell.

If I'd known medicines like these, maybe I could have saved my mother?

The question lingered in her mind. This was something she could learn from the Angu, if only she made her peace with them. Maybe none of the stories were true? She stood and clambered out into the cool early morning air.

A tall, wiry man sprang to his feet. His eyeglasses glinted in the morning light. He looked solemnly at Ari, brandishing a long spear.

△△△

The man's bare chest was a dark network of wiry muscles. Beneath the thick eyeglasses, the whites of his enlarged eyes were in vivid contrast with his tanned face. A crooked scar worked its way across the bottom of his jaw and his hands were large with round knuckles and long fingers that gripped the pole of the spear.

Ari had the impulse to reach for her blade. Her hand danced delicately in the air, ready to pounce. She looked into the man's solemn eyes, but the eyeglasses robbed them of their menace.

The man took a step closer and levelled his spear with her.

"We gonna do this?" said Ari.

The man didn't respond.

There was a crashing noise from inside one of the nearby huts, along with what sounded like the twittering of birds. Jirra appeared at the hut's entrance and squashed his bush hat over his mop of black hair. His round pendant flashed in the morning sun. He looked about himself as if slightly confused and then looked at Ari. "Ya drink?"

"Yeah," replied Ari.

"Ya friend drink?"

"Yeah."

Jirra grinned. "Goodonya. She wake?"

"A little."

He turned to the wiry figure with the spear. "Doug, she be right."

The man lowered his spear but still eyed Ari suspiciously.

Jirra scurried over to the hut where Ari and Starla had spent the night. He hitched open the curtain and went inside. Ari followed him. In the dim light, he knelt down and undid Starla's dressing. He cleared out the leaves and petals but left the maggots. Much of the yellow pus was already gone.

"Ya see," said the man, indicating to the wound. "They eat the yella stuff." He redressed the wound and went back outside. Ari followed him.

"She gonna be okay?" she asked.

"She'll be right," Jirra said. "A few days an' she'll be right."

Ari nodded. "Look, why ya helpin' us?"

The man scrunched up his forehead. "Ya friend not well."

"Yeah, but what's it to ya?"

The man scratched his chin, then he turned to the horizon and pointed over the top of the oval huts to a big red rock standing on its own.

"That rock."

"Yeah."

"That the rock of the village. Folks call it sacred. So Maka put that there, an' Maka put us 'ere. Maka put ya in the valley but he put the emu-bush 'ere. Ya see? "

Ari wasn't really sure what the man was talking about.

"Ya friend not well," Jirra continued. "We'll put 'er back the way Maka wants it."

Ari sucked on the bottom of her lip. "Well, thanks anyway."

The man scratched his chin again. Briefly, he looked as if he was rolling an idea around in his mind, then he shook his head. He patted Ari on the back.

"She'll be right."

CHAPTER 25

Starla stood in a patch of long grass by a bare gum-tree; before her was an oval-shaped hut, simple and formed from wood and mud. Above, the sky was turning purple. The long grass tickled her bare legs. Starla watched as a tiny child, cradled in the arms of an old woman in a heavy shawl, was carried into the hut. She began to hobble towards the hut's dark entrance. She needed to get the child back. Her leg hurt. From inside the hut, she could hear the baby crying.

I'm coming, she thought. But her leg was growing stiff and it was harder and harder to move it.

Then, in a plume of orange fire, the hut exploded.

Starla awakened gasping. Her heart thumped against her ribcage like a bird ready to escape.

A bird that was, for now, still caged.

It was only a dream.

It was dark in the hut and it smelt rich and musty. Starla rolled off her bed and a sharp pain surged up her leg.

She dragged herself to her feet and made her way to the entrance of the hut. Outside, men and woman had formed a chain, moving brown sacks into a hut opposite. They had the heavily tanned skin of the outsiders, some so dark it almost seemed black. They wore the well-worn rags of the outsiders too, though some were bare chested. Around their necks, some wore strings of coloured beads.

Where am I now, she wondered.

She became dizzy and dark spots formed in her vision. She leant her forehead against the doorway of the hut.

Gradually, she let herself sink to her knees.

△△△

Over the coming days, Starla began to improve. After two days, she was awake more often, and for longer, and after a week she was moving around the village on a crutch. Ari brought her food and drink but would also disappear for whole days into the bush with other villagers to hunt for lizards and kangaroos or forage for bush coconuts and grubs. This existence seemed to please Ari. She wasn't quite as thin now and her pale eyes looked brighter. She smiled more often and slept soundly on the floor of the hut beside Starla, and Starla began to wonder if Ari would actually like to remain in the village indefinitely.

One afternoon, at the edge of the village, Starla took a seat under a gumtree in the shade. Once on the ground, she stretched out her throbbing leg and winced. Insects chattered in the dry grass.

Maggots, she thought. How could I let them put maggots in my wound?

Between two huts, she watched a group of boys and girls playing with a ball. They were kicking it between themselves and laughing to each other. Then two boys tripped each other over and a half-hearted argument broke out. Starla could barely understand what any of them were saying, the accent here was so much stronger than Ari's.

A pain shot down her leg. Starla began to massage the top of the calf. In the city, her leg would have been fixed with a day in a medi-ray machine; a tedious day, but nothing more arduous.

Maggots, seriously.

And bitten by a crocodile. Starved, parched, threatened, chased by dingoes and half drowned. I should be in the city. I should be in my room, ordering syntho. I don't belong here. These people don't even know who I am.

But does who I am really matter?

The thought surprised her. She stopped massaging her leg and examined her hands, turning them over. They were dark and blotchy. Where they peeled, underneath the skin was red and raw. Her nails were blunt and uneven. Around her cuticles, the last residuals of her blue nail varnish still clung on, a final reminder of her other life. She was turning into an outsider. Her skin was ruined. She didn't even have a mirror, which was probably lucky. She ran her fingers through her dark hair and it felt brittle and shapeless.

A tear rolled down her cheek and she wiped it away quickly and sniffed.

Maybe I'm glad not to have a mirror, she thought.

The children's laughter distracted her and she looked up. They were running after each other, the ball bouncing between their legs.

A week, she thought. It's been at least a week. And I can barely walk. What if I end up stuck here?

A heat rose in her gut.

But what if I did, she thought.

She remembered the glass tower that had been home for so long.

I felt like a prisoner. I was pushed around, controlled. What if I go back and I'm a prisoner again? And why haven't I been rescued?

She scanned the pale sky. Would they come by land or air? If they'd come at all.

It seemed unlikely now, and day by day the city was becoming more and more like fantasy. She pressed the points on the inside of her arm.

Maybe there is no telephone, perhaps I

dreamed it up.

Then she found the tiny scar left by the implant.

If I go back, things will have to change. I won't be pushed around. I'll stand on my own two feet, or I'll be able to soon.

She began to massage her leg again and remembered leaping into the water to save Ari.

I did that.

And what about Ari? She's happier here. Maybe she no longer wants to go back to the city? Could I make it on my own from here... Not yet, but when my leg is better?

A lump formed in her throat and the heat in her gut subsided.

Maybe I could make it? If that's what Ari wants.

Under the tree, Starla felt small and alone and the children playing seemed miles away, like the alien beings of another race and time. For a moment, she had the feeling of disappearing entirely. It was as if her dark, blotchy skin was melting into the faded bark of the gumtree, and with it all the elements that once defined her small, confined existence at the top of the glass tower.

△△△

Ari balanced the wooden spear between her fingers and thumb, neither end heavier than the other, just as Doug had shown her. One blackened end was sharpened to a point. She moved quietly through the long, dry grass. Downwind, she could smell the faint, spicy scent of the kangaroo. Something cracked underfoot; the animal's head shot up, grey hair prickled. It rolled its jaw, beady eyes searching the scrubland. It saw her but didn't see her. Ari remained still.

The kangaroo dipped its head again and pulled at the long grass stems.

Gently, Ari raised her left arm forward, lining her empty hand with her prey. She drew the spear back with her right, twisting her body, ready to spring.

Left foot forwards, right knee bent.

She spun forwards like a wheel and released the spear.

The weapon flew quickly, in a shallow arch through the dry air. It fell short of its target.

The animal took flight, bounding erratically through the long grass. Ari took chase, dry blades dragging and cracking against her legs.

She reached her spear and grasped it as she ran.

Doug was moving through the grass too, his dark body a web of silent, rolling muscles, eyeglasses glinting in the sun.

The kangaroo leapt towards the tree line. If he made it, they'd lose him in the dense gumtrees.

Ari rolled her body backward, left arm forward, right arm back, and threw again.

The spear landed just a tail from its target.

The animal changed direction, moving up hill again, its body bouncing above and below the line of the long grass.

Doug pulled his spear back and threw.

The spear spun in a high arch, descending fast and striking home.

The kangaroo released a short, gravel like bark and went down on its side, the spear sticking upright from its belly like the pole of a victory flag. It gently moved with the rise and fall of the animal's chest.

Ari ran to the fallen prey.

The kangaroo panted erratically, sticky red blood trickling from where the spear went in. It looked at her with wild, fiery eyes, perhaps recognising now what it had casually discarded before.

Doug appeared by her side, holding a spear upright.

Ari knelt by the animal. Her hands shook. She took the blade from her ankle and, one hand resting on its warm, muscular neck, she slit the animal's throat. The spicy scent mingled with the metallic tang of blood.

"An' now," said Doug, "he return to the earth."

"I shoulda had 'im," said Ari.

She wiped the blade on the animal's grey fur and slipped it back in its sheath at her ankle.

"This kinda thin' takes practice," said Doug. Holding the spear upright in his elbow, he removed his eyeglasses and began to rub them on his shorts.

"Whatever," said Ari. "I coulda got 'im if ya hadn't butt in."

Doug shook his head. "Na, ya couldn', ya needed another spear."

He showed Ari the end of the spear he was holding. It was Ari's spear. The end, burnt black and sharpened to a point, was broken.

"Musta hit a rock," he said. "Ya can sharpen it again."

Ari sighed. She pulled Doug's spear from the carcass and they bound the animal's limbs around the two spears to carry it back to the village. As Doug led the way, the head of the spears over his shoulder, Ari sulked.

I shoulda had him. I missed him last time too. Next time I'll get him.

The animal's head dragged limply against the long grass. Its eyes were open but the fire had gone. Twisted now, in an unnatural position, it was hard to imagine the carcass had ever held life.

In the city they eat syntho, she thought. And they don't have to catch it, or go hungry because they can't. It's just there to be eaten. They live in rooms with roofs and walls and fireplaces, or whatever the city folk actually have to keep them warm. And they eat whenever they want to. And that's what I'll do when I get to the city.

She tried to visualise her lost home in the city, the rooms with the purple light, the balcony overlooking a mechanical forest of steel and glass.

The image seemed hazier now, as if Starla's descriptions of the city had begun to rearrange her own memories. She thought of the purple powder on her mother's dressing table, she knew she'd seen this. Then she remembered her mother's lifeless eyes, staring up at the ceiling of the hut.

She was staring into the eyes of the dead kangaroo.

And next time I'll have him, she thought. And Doug will have to drop that condescending tone.

$$\triangle \triangle \triangle$$

Later, they lay on the floor of their hut, the fire crackling in the hearth.

Starla rolled onto her side on the small bed she'd been provided. "Why do you want to go to the city?"

Ari looked up from the floor, where she lay on a blanket, and her pale eyes caught the flames of the fire. "What do ya mean?"

"You seem happy here. I worry sometimes how you'll find the city."

"But I'm from Alice."

"You were, maybe you're not anymore though. You know, no one in the city calls it Alice."

Ari looked back at the ceiling. "I remember the parks. Big green places where ya could run or climb an' still feel safe. An' never bein' hungry.

An' all the people were so beautiful. Ya know." Ari looked at Starla. "A place like that's for anyone."

"What else do you remember?"

"I remember the lights at night, in every colour ya could think of. An' the buildings. An' everythin' bein' so clean all the time."

"I guess. But being away from it, in a place like this. It's made me realise things. In the city, people might not like you."

"I don' care about that. People are the same all over I reckon. Some ya can trust, an' some ya can't. Can't trust no one in Cooper, that's for sure." Ari smiled. "Well, maybe Wheels, but that's only cause he can't run."

"In the city they hate outsiders. Pretty much the only ones are people who've only visited the outside. Just visit and you're marked." Starla briefly paused, then said, "I guess I'm marked now... But people who've lived out here? And even if you're not an outsider, you have to live by the rules. You have to fit into the social order. You have to say and think all the right things all the time. I guess I worry about you after seeing you here."

Ari looked at Starla. "Ya don't want me to come?"

"It's not that, just, I worry."

"Look sister, if ya don't want me to come ya just say. But we had a deal ya know."

"No, really, it's not that."

Ari sat up. "We had a deal."

"We still do."

"Then what?"

Starla sighed. "It's just…"

"We had a deal so ya can save it." Ari got to her feet and stormed out of the hut.

What is her problem? I'm just concerned, that's all.

Starla got up from her bed and hobbled into the darkness. A short way from the hut, Ari sat on a rock. The dark silhouette of the rocky hills were just discernible in the moonlight. Starla hobbled over and sat on the rock next to Ari. Ari thrust something back into her pocket, as if she didn't want Starla to see what she'd been holding. For a moment they were silent. Starla shivered and drew her arms around herself.

Finally, Ari spoke.

"I remember in the city I was never hungry. But in Cooper I was never not hungry. Ya can't think when ya hungry. Hungry people can't do nothin' else but be hungry. I don' wanna be hungry no more."

Starla reached out and took Ari's hand. It felt warm.

"Hungry people can't build no city," Ari continued. "Only work they can do is dig up salt for the city, and they don't see nothin' for it but a bit 'a stale bread. In Cooper I's just waitin' to give up all hope an' join the slave drivers in the ore mines. They say they feed ya there, but no one ever comes back." Ari sighed. "There's no hope stayin' in Cooper. No future. Just hunger an' salt an' more hunger. And…"

"What?"

"It's just, I ain't had much to hope for, not in a long time, not till…"

"I'm sorry," said Starla. "I didn't mean anything by what I said. I honestly didn't. I want you to come. I want us both to go to the city. When my leg's better we'll go."

Ari turned to Starla and her eyes caught the moonlight. "Good, cause ya ain't stoppin' me now sister."

CHAPTER 26

Max surveyed the swamp from the aircraft window. A long, brown river snaked through dense, green foliage. Much of the land was hidden under the forest canopy. These were tribal lands, but they were also the source of the city's water supply.

The aircraft flew low, following the course of the river as it cut through valleys and around rocks. Long shingle beaches flanked the river.

There had to be signs of people breaking ground somewhere. Would people from Cooper come here?

It was impossible to say, nothing of the people on the outside made sense. It was just as use, entrusting a task to a pigeon. But if they were to get back to the road, they'd have to cut across the swamp. Max was sure he was close.

△△△

One evening, Starla and Ari went over to Jirra's hut to announce their intention to depart. From outside the hut, Ari called in.

"Jirra."

The curtain was pulled aside and Jirra beckoned them in with a grin and a sideways dip of his head.

Ari went ahead and, after a moments hesitation, Starla hobbled behind, ducking to get through the low door.

In the centre of the hut, the suspended oil lamp gave off a rich, fatty smell. In the orange glow, ancient books, musty volumes like the ones left unread in the city archives, had been stacked floor to ceiling. A patterned curtain covered what must have been his sleeping quarters. Against one side of the hut were several square, metal cages, inside which hopped numerous tiny yellow and green birds. They twittered to each other, fidgeting with quick, delicate movements.

"The birds," said Starla.

"Yeah," said Jirra grinning. "These are my little ones."

He took a small, brown bag and from it he began pushing small seeds through the bars to the birds. They hopped towards his fingers, plucking up the seeds. He held the bag out to Starla.

"Ya wanna?"

Starla hesitated a moment, then took a few seeds from the bag. She poked a seed through the tiny bars. A small, yellow bird hopped forward and plucked it from her fingers. It looked at her sideways with shiny black eyes, puffed its belly, and hopped away. Starla pushed more seeds through the bars and more birds skipped towards her.

"See," said Jirra. "They like ya."

"They like ya seeds," said Ari.

Starla ignored her and poked the last of her seeds through the bars. "What kind of birds are these?"

"Canaries," said Jirra. "I like 'em. Somethin' reassurin' about 'em I reckon. They's workin' birds. Folks take 'em down the mines."

"Why?" asked Starla.

"The air down the mine," said Jirra. "If ya canary dies, ya know you'll be next if ya don't get up top quick. Beside, I like how canaries sing."

"So anyway," said Ari. "We gotta go soon. Got places to be."

"Yeah, I figured," said Jirra. "Ya need to get to Alice. We'll take ya far as the dam. Then ya nearly there."

"We know the way," said Ari.

"Yeah," said Jirra. "But ya friend ain't strong." He nodded towards Starla. "We'll make sure ya right."

Ari looked down at her feet and sucked at the bottom of her lip.

"We accept your help," said Starla.

Ari shot her a glance.

"But we must go soon," said Starla.

Whatever it takes, she thought, we need to leave.

Jirra nodded. "But first, before ya go an' leave, I've somethin' I need to show ya. We can go now."

Jirra led them outside into the cool, dark night. Above, the canvas of stars twinkled. He led the way, out of the village and towards the big red rock. Following behind, Starla winced as her leg throbbed. They passed the rock and began to follow a path up a shallow hill.

"No huntin' this way," said Jirra. "They keeps it sacred. But we'll be right."

"Are we goin' far?" asked Ari.

"No, not far."

"What about Starla's leg?"

"It ain't far," repeated Jirra, "an' if ya friend ain't up to it, she ain't ready to leave the village."

"I'm fine," said Starla.

"See, she'll be right."

For some time, they trudged upwards towards the crest of the hill.

Not far, thought Starla. This isn't what I'd call not far, but I have to leave this place. If this is what it takes...

Finally, they reached the crest. Below, glowing in the moonlight, was a vast, silver bowl, hollowed into the land. Perfectly round, it was the size of small lake. From four corners of the bowl ran steel cables, and in the centre, as if suspended from the cables, was a complicated triangular structure of boxes and pipes.

"We're headin' there," said Jirra, pointing towards the suspended structure.

"What is this place?" asked Ari.

"We call this the dish," said Jirra. He led them to a metal walkway that ran above the dish and creaked underfoot.

"This thin' safe?" asked Ari.

"Don' worry," said Jirra. "Its been 'ere a long time."

Who's worried, thought Starla. Following behind, she hobbled up the steps and onto the walkway.

"Ya okay?" asked Ari.

"I told you, I'm fine," said Starla. She looked down from the walkway, far below to the concave bottom of the dish, and felt dizzy. She imagined herself falling and rolling down the vast, smooth surface, all the way to the bottom. The surface seemed barely blemished, as if it was purposefully kept clear of the encroaching jungle.

They reached the structure in the centre and Jirra led them through a dark doorway. Starla could hear him fumbling in the gloom and she deliberately stayed close to the doorway. Then the cream glow of an electric light revealed a small room full of panels and switches. Cables ran everywhere, often bound together five or ten at a time. Gradually, the dials and switches began to glow. A large screen illuminated on the wall, projecting an image of a night sky.

"Here," said Jirra, "we can talk to the stars."

"Wha' do ya mean?" asked Ari.

Starla lowered herself onto a chair by a panel and stretched out her leg.

"Me Dad brought me 'ere," said Jirra. "He showed me how to move the dish, to point it to the different stars. Today, mostly, the stars are silent. It had been the same for me Dad. Long ago maybe, all the stars talked, now they only hiss. Some pulse, like they may be machines, but they don' talk. None except one."

Jirra walked around the panel and pointed to the star in the centre of the screen.

Starla burst out, "Velle Stella."

Ari looked at her. "Vella what?"

"Velle Stella," repeated Starla. "The star that never moves."

"Ain't heard it called that before," said Ari.

"We call it the Maka star," said Jirra.

I think I prefer Velle Stella, thought Starla. It sounds more like Starla.

Magnified on the screen, the star shone faintly blue.

"But ya right," said Jirra. "The star that don' move. The sun, the moon, all the other stars, they move right across the sky, but not this one. This one stay put, day an' night. Even by day, when we can' see it, we know it's there. We can still talk to it usin' the dish."

Jirra moved around the panels and began turning a series of dials. A speaker somewhere began to hiss.

"Now ya can 'ear the silence of the stars," said Jirra.

The hiss modulated.

It's just sounds like static, thought Starla.

"This sound is all they make now. The sound's not always the same, but still it's always the same. But listen…"

He gently turned a dial on the panel. At first there was only the hiss, sometimes pulsing, sometimes droning, and then a thin, crackly voice appeared. It was a man's voice.

"…one final time before the impact. The meteorite which, for the past nine years, organisations around the globe have tirelessly tracked, will impact the eastern seaboard at approximately 11:46 EST. We understand that, due to the angle of the approach, and the speed with which it is travelling, the most likely consequence of this impact will be a change in this planet's orbit. God willing, this change will not be too great. In the short term, the planet will most likely be covered in a large dust cloud. Some regions will experience an unseasonal winter. During this period, stay in your shelters and avoid all unnecessary travel. When outside, wear your mask, and cover all exposed skin. Ration your food and fuel. Care for yourselves and your loved ones. Check on your neighbours. Community has never been more important than it is now. In the long term, the environment and the seasons of this planet may be permanently changed. The planet

of the future may be one quite different from the one we have known up until now. But, my fellow citizens, know this. We will endure. Our species will survive, of this I have no doubt. Our courage and our ingenuity will ensure our place in whatever world we find ourselves. Until then, go to your shelters. Hold your loved ones close. And may God help us in our most desperate hour. Our generation, and the generations that follow, will meet the greatest challenge we, as a species, have ever endured. But we will rebuild our world. We will make it again. And we will put the things back, not as they are now, but as the way they should be. Perhaps we can build a world without borders, a world without walls. A kinder, more caring world, that shares with all the fruits of our endeavours, where one person can stand equal to another. So, my fellow citizens, as I speak to you this final time, that is the message I wish to leave you with. My hope that a better world can be born from our heavy sacrifice. That future will be up to you, and the world will be what you make it. Now, I wish you all good night and good luck. I shall join my loved ones and there I shall pray. Tomorrow, the world shall be very different. God bless us all."

Following the message, a tune was performed on brass instruments. Starla looked up at Ari, who was chewing at the bottom of her lip, and then across the Jirra.

"I don' understand," said Ari.

"A meteorite," said Starla.

"What's one'a them?" asked Ari.

"It's a rock that falls from space," said Starla.

The tune stopped and the message began to repeat.

"My fellow citizens, it is with a heavy heart that I address you now, one final time before the impact. The meteorite…"

Jirra silenced the voice. "The star that speaks."

Starla massaged her leg. "The message sounds like it started out here on the ground."

"Yeah," said Jirra. "Sometime I think this. But the way I figure, Maka speaks to us in many ways. And surely, only Maka could put it there, so high in the sky."

"In the city," said Starla, "there are stories of people long ago who visited the stars. People could have put it there. Probably the same people who built this dish even."

Jirra stroked his beard. "Perhaps."

"I don' think that voice sounded like the Maka," said Ari.

"What does the voice of the Maka sound like?" asked Jirra.

"Dunno. Not like that though. I don't think the Maka needs words see. Ya feel 'im."

Jirra grinned. "It's like I say. Maka speaks to us in many ways." He raised his finger to Ari. "Ya sound like the shaman. He tells me somethin' very like this. But if this be, Maka comes to me like this. I grew up in the bush, not in the city. But without this place, I couldn' believe in no Maka. I could believe in the emu bush an' the old wisdom, but in no Maka. But then I 'ear this voice, I know Maka finds 'is way with even me. When my father found the Maka star spoke, he were shunned by the shaman. I am shunned too. But he's a nice man, the shaman. He like my canaries. Bein' shunned ain't so bad."

"Why did you bring us here?" asked Starla.

"To show ya," said Jirra. "So ya can 'ear for ya self before ya go to Alice. See, people don't go from 'ere to the city. Not till you. Ya can take this message to them. No more walls. Maka wants things back where they belong, the way they shoulda been always. And that means no more walls."

CHAPTER 27

Starla was still limping when they left the Angu village and began their journey onwards towards the city. Ari watched her cautiously. Ari wasn't convinced she wanted the Angu as guides, but at least they might be some protection. After all, she had almost gotten Starla killed.

In all, there were five of them; Ari and Starla, Jirra and Doug, and Koora. Doug and Koora carried heavy sacks on their backs and spears in their hands. Jirra had his satchel, his round pendant hung from his neck and his bush hat wedged over his black hair.

On their first day, they made for the river and traced it at a distance through the valley. In the heat, the landscape grew drier and more arid again. They said little, their heads lowered. Ari watched the bulky packs wobbling on Doug's and Koora's backs.

The city, she thought. Ain't no reason we

won't make it now. Not as long as Starla can keep going. And then there's syntho and four walls and a roof.

She reached inside her pocket and felt the bristles of the lashes. Did anyone still know her, on the other side of the wall? Some long forgotten relative. They probably wouldn't recognise her now, but still... maybe.

In the late afternoon, they made camp next to a group of large, red rocks. While Koora and Doug set about building a fire, Jirra beckoned to Ari and Starla. He led them along a worn path that cut through the rocks, to the entrance of a dark cave.

"I think ya'll find this interestin'," he said.

A cool breeze flowed up from the cave. At the back, breaking through from some chamber beyond, penetrated a thin ray of yellow light.

"Where's it go?" asked Ari.

"Ya'll see," said Jirra, going ahead into the cave.

Ari looked at Starla and Starla shrugged. Well, she thought, we don't have nothing to lose I guess.

Ari followed Jirra and she heard Starla limping behind.

The back of the cave opened into a large grotto with a high ceiling. Far above, a round aperture allowed a solid shaft of sunlight to illuminate one vast wall of red rock. Every part of this wall was covered in primitive looking drawings. Many overlapped, while others crowded to fit around each other. There were what looked like people and animals, buildings and trees; there were hand prints and spiral shapes and symbols of every kind. Some were small but others were huge. They were scratched onto the wall, or printed or painted, in black or red or white.

"What is this?" asked Ari, as her eyes worked their way up the rock face.

"This," said Jirra, "is the story of the world as our shaman sees it."

Ari's eyes widened. She'd never seen anything like this before, that was, if she didn't count the images she'd drawn onto the wall of her own cave. "Who made this?"

"Folks who came before us. We just found it. Now we keeps it safe, just as it is. Look here." He pointed to a red figure, outlined in white, with a face that featured two big, white eyes. "This is the start. He comes from the sky, from the Maka star. First he makes day an' night, an' then he makes rivers an' trees. He makes the animals, an' he makes the people."

Jirra pointed to images of people running and people hunting and many different animals, some of which Ari could recognise, like kangaroos and crocodiles.

Ari gasped. "It's amazin'."

She wondered how these people had drawn it. She wanted to take up a bit of the black rock and add her own images to it.

Jirra pointed to the images of tall buildings and what looked like vehicles and aircraft.

"Ya see, Maka builds cities everywhere. He makes the roads an' he makes light when it's dark. All the things he makes, he gives to us. See, he makes cars an' he makes machines. All of these things, they were put underground an' we brought them up."

"You can't believe that," said Starla.

Jirra grinned. "I didn' say I did. But this is how the shaman sees it. An' ya know, perhaps it ain't so wrong."

"And what about the city?" asked Starla. "There aren't cities everywhere. There's only one."

"Well, ya see, at first everyone shared the world. But then things changed, people stopped the sharing, they built walls, and instead of peace there was war." He pointed to images of flames and people burning, and then to a mountain with what looked like fire and smoke bursting from its summit. "This was not how Maka wants it, and so thunder came from the skies an' the world turned to fire. The mountains exploded an' the rivers flowed with flames an' all was lost. And now the world is broken."

"Or a meteorite struck the planet," said Starla.

"Perhaps Maka sent the meteorite," said Jirra. "Folks who made this, they saw it as they saw it. But ya from Alice. Ya must see Maka is still angry with us. That's why the message from the Maka star is so important." He pointed back to the wall. "We must put it all back as it's meant to be. Otherwise, there can be no more cities, not even Alice. There can be no more division. No more breaks in the world. We must take down the wall or the city will die."

△△△

As they left the cave, Starla hung behind. Ari got a little ahead and then turned back.

"Ya okay?"

Starla shrugged. She dropped onto the ground and began to massage her leg. "These people are crazy." Dizzy, she rested her head against her knee.

Ari knelt down beside her. "I dunno. Maybe they know somethin' we don't."

"I don't trust them."

"Well, I don't trust no one." Ari glanced back at the three men. "But I kinda trust 'em a little more 'an I trust most folk."

"Back there, he was talking like he thinks it's my fault for the world dying or something. But we all heard the same message. And you know what, the people in the city are just trying to survive too. We're all the same."

"He didn' mean it like that. Just, well, I never took much stock in the Maka. I never felt I needed too. But these guys? They put a lot 'a stock in 'im. They wanna know what happened to the world. I never cared that much, world is what the world is. But I dunno, maybe I shoulda'."

Starla rolled her eyes. "Just know they can't come in the city. That's not part of our deal."

"Well," said Ari. "It's just as far as the dam. Then we're almost there. An' we gotta better chance of makin' it with these guys." Ari smiled sheepishly. "See, I nearly got ya killed. An' then what would I do?"

CHAPTER 28

The following afternoon, they made sight of the dam. The lazy river took a long meander and, between the two channels, the party cut across the rocks. At a high vantage, they looked down on the wide metal structure, rusty and tired, at the mouth of the river. It was hard to imagine it was still functioning. On one side a bulb of water was held back, while on the other water gushed down a series of metal channels into the basin below at the end of the valley. From here, the water cut hard into the open plain before it disappeared into an underground channel that flowed to the city. After that, the landscape between the swamp and the city was a dry and lifeless desert. The old course of the river was just visible as a shallow, dry channel.

In the middle of the dam sat a small metal building and beside it a hexagonal-shaped landing platform, faded markings in red and white still visible on its smooth surface.

The party made their way down the rocks towards the dam. Half way down, a path had been marked out. The metal plates creaked underfoot. In places, the brown rust had eaten deep into the ancient metal and patches of the path would disintegrate underfoot with a satisfying crunch.

A short way from the dam, Starla felt a mild vibration from her left elbow to her wrist. She looked down just as the yellow light beneath the skin faded. Her heart leapt. She pressed the spot on her forearm and the familiar yellow and blue lights blinked. Instinctively, she pressed the communication button and raised her palm.

The Angu men had gone ahead but Ari hung back.

"Hello," said the robotic voice of the operator.

She felt her cheeks flush while her fingers started to go numb. She let out a brief, nervous laugh.

"Excuse me, Miss Corinth," said the operator. "I..."

The operator was silent for a moment, as if afraid of interrupting the first daughter of the city.

"I'm at the dam," Starla managed.

"Yes, Miss Corinth," said the operator. "And it is an honour Miss, and don't worry, we have your position. We're sending a rescue craft. Just stay where you are."

The signal broke and the lights on her arm

faded. Starla exhaled slowly and the right corner of her lip curling upwards. "We made it," she said. "They're coming."

Ari looked at her warily. "They're comin' 'ere?"

"Yes. We just have to stay where we are, they're on their way."

Ari wiped the sweat off her shaven head and looked about. The Angu had disappeared onto the dam. "The city, eh."

"Yes." Starla's heart skipped and the pain in her leg faded. She ran forward and hugged Ari. Ari's arms stayed limp at her sides. "We're going home. And you made it happen."

"Yeah," said Ari.

"What's the matter?"

"Nothin'," said Ari and she grinned uneasily. "Just a lot to take, ya know."

"You'll love it Ari, I know you will."

"Yeah, I guess." Ari looked back towards the dam. "I wonder where they've got to." She pulled away from Starla and continued along the path towards the dam.

Tonight, thought Starla, I'll shower and eat syntho cubes. Maybe I'll eat purple, or green, or blue. The sudden possibilities seemed endless.

Ari reached the metal steps and began to climb. Starla followed. The steps creaked underfoot. At the top, pockmarked with rusty welts, was a walkway that seemed run the length of the dam. Water roared beneath them, churning up a cool spray. The Angu men were up ahead. A platform ran beneath the walkway and Doug had climbed down to it. Koora was on his knees, emptying the sack he'd been carrying. Jirra seemed to be inspecting the channels than ran out from the dam.

They approached the men and Ari asked, "What ya doin'?"

Jirra looked up at her and grinned. "We're puttin' things back, just as Maka wants it."

"Puttin' things back?"

△△△

In the distance, beyond the horizon, a winged air-craft approached low. It banked over the wide, flat plain as it adjusted course for the dam.

△△△

"Puttin' things back," confirmed Jirra. "The dam is destroyin' the land. It's ruinin' the river."

△△△

The aircraft began it's decent, black wings dipped forwards.

△△△

From somewhere in the distance, a low hum grew louder.

"So?" asked Ari.

"So, now we use the fire powder to blow it up."

CHAPTER 29

Jirra's eyes looked wild and excited.

These people are crazy, thought Ari. All this talk about putting things back the way the Maker wants it, and now they want to blow the dam? But it's only fair I warn them. They'd do that for us.

"That aircraft," she said, and pointed at the humming black dot that grew larger in the clear blue sky. "That's from the city."

Jirra raised his eyebrows. "Then we'll work faster."

"Look," said Ari. "Don' blow this thing till they've gone, right."

"They come 'ere for ya?"

"Yeah, they're our ride. But ya blow this now an' ya gonna ruin it for us."

Jirra nodded. "No worries. We know what we're doin'."

That's what I'm afraid of, thought Ari.

Koora was down on the platform below, running a cord along the length of the dam. Doug was planting packages at regular intervals, close to the channels.

"Come on," she said to Starla.

They left Jirra lowering packages down to Doug and headed for the small building in the middle of the dam. A flight of stairs led to a small room with windows that must have once held glass. Inside, the dusty panels still emitted a low hum. Starla reached forward and cleared red dust from a round, glass dial. Below the dial, a tiny red light still glowed.

"Ya know what this place is?" asked Ari.

Starla shook her head.

"Whatever it is, it's still doin' something."

Through the window, Ari watched the men as they walked the length of the dam, seemingly inspecting their work. They better know what they're doing, she thought. This place better not explode with us still on it.

The aircraft drew closer. Through the empty windows, its large, black shape took form in the pale blue sky; nose dipped, two broad wings with holes in their centres, and a forked tail. Hovering in the air, it reminded Ari of a poised scorpion. Ari had never been in an aircraft before. She watched it come down close to the dam, sunlight glinting on its glazed cockpit. The rumbling noise got louder and louder until it drowned out the sound of the water rushing beneath them through the dam.

ThwopThwopThwopThwopThwop...

The aircraft banked overhead and circled the dam.

"What's it doin'?" asked Ari over the din.

Starla shook her head. "I don't know."

The aircraft slowed to a hover and gently circled above the dam. Then it opened fire.

△△△

Bullets ricocheted across the top of the dam. The guns on the aircraft made a rattling fop-fop sound.

Ari and Starla dropped to the floor and hid beneath the open windows. Ari peered nervously over the top of the sill. Koora was lying face down on the bottom platform. He wasn't moving. Jirra and Doug were running along the top of the dam. The aircraft's nose followed them. Bullets hit the deck of the dam like tiny bursts of steam. Jirra fell to the floor and rolled over. Doug kept running and made it to the riverbank. Ari dropped back down behind the windowsill.

"They shot them."

"Who?"

"The Angu."

The aircraft's guns paused. Its propellers thundered and the cabin vibrated as the aircraft moved directly overhead.

"What now?" asked Ari.

"I don't know."

They must have thought the Angu had abducted Starla, thought Ari. So what's to stop them also shooting me? These are people from the city, they don't care about anyone else. She thought of Jirra and Koora. That wasn't fair. How could they just shoot them like that? A lump formed in her throat. She wanted to get up and see if they were alive. The longer they lay unattended, the less likely that'd be. Perhaps I could revive them. I could find emu-bush in Jirra's satchel and press it into their wounds. I could save them.

The engines rumbled as the aircraft manoeuvred into a hovering position over the landing platform. Ari watched it cautiously.

And how could I get on that aircraft now, after I've watched it cut down our friends? And even if I did, they'd probably lift into the air and then throw me out the door.

Ari imagined the fall through the empty air, only to hit the dead earth with a thud.

Briefly, the black form hung in the air, its undercarriage unfolding, then it gently dropped down. With a high, unwinding sound, the engines slowed, then fell silent. Ari tugged Starla and they shuffled into a hiding position under the panels. Ari's heart thumped against her breastbone.

Beyond the panel, a heavy clank came from the direction of landing platform, then footsteps; boots on a metallic surface.

Ari looked at Starla. This was Starla's world now. These were Starla's people, this was Starla's plan. But Starla's eyes were wide, her forehead frozen, the colour drained from her cheeks. She didn't look like she had a plan.

A male voice rang out across the landing platform.

"Starla, where are you?"

Starla raised her eyebrows and, when she spoke, it was almost a whisper. "That's Max."

CHAPTER 30

Max was on the landing platform.

Starla wondered, is he here to rescue me?

But he'd just gunned down the Angu. Why had he done that?

Not long ago, she'd wished for Max to rescue her, now she wondered why he had come at all. Now, time was collapsing, and the birthday party felt like only yesterday. Now, her time on the outside felt like a dream; some horrible nightmare from which she was only now waking. And with this coming morning came the instinctive feeling that Max was not a man to be trusted. Max was from the Panache family, her family's closest allies and biggest rivals.

"Ya know 'im?" asked Ari.

Starla nodded. "Yes."

"Who is he?"

Starla paused. "Someone from the city."

"Well?"

"Stay here."

Ari nodded.

A chill came over Starla and her palms began to sweat. Slowly, she stood and looked out through the window towards the landing platform. Max stood in front of the large, black aircraft. His blue jacket billowed in the warm breeze. He was flanked, on either side, by two members of the praetorian guard in blue uniforms, their faces covered by dark visors, and they each carried a large gun.

Max took a step forward and his green eyes glinted. "Starla Corinth, you know the hardest thing about finding you was making it look this easy." He grinned sideways.

Starla inched around the panel to the doorway and stepped out onto the platform. She cleared her throat. "What are you doing here Max?"

Max's smile widened. "Starla, I'm taking you back to Cooper. What do you think? I'm here to take you back to the city."

"Really."

"Honestly. Now come before I change my mind."

"Why you?"

"Why not?"

"Why you, and not someone from my father."

"Starla..." For a moment Max seemed to be trying to find the words. "I'm here because your father sent me. We are family Starla. And you being lost out here, that goes beyond any petty family feuds. Out here we stick together. And you and I. We're the future Starla."

But Starla didn't trust it. Something wasn't right. She looked at the wide open door of the aircraft and it looked like the jaws of some great animal. Maybe she was seeing things, maybe she'd been out here far too long, unable to feel safe or trust in anything or anyone, but her deepest primal instincts were reignited; she wanted to fight or she wanted to flee.

Now it seemed like a long time since the night of the party, so many moons ago. She remembered Liviana standing too closely on the balcony. She remembered the way she spilled the blue champagne…

∆∆∆

When he'd heard Starla was missing, Max's father had been furious.

"We can't leverage Corinth if we don't know where she is, now can we?"

Red-faced, he'd paced back and forth in his office, rubbing his palms against his thighs.

"Those bogans are useless," Max had said. He'd pulled at the skin on the back of his neck. Sweat clung to his brow. "Bunch of inbreed swamp-rats."

Agrippa Panache had stopped pacing and had

affixed his unblinking gaze on Max.

"No. It's you, my boy, who's useless. They haven't lost her, you have. The buck stops with you, you hear me? I didn't authorise this. This, my boy, is all you. It's in your hands now."

"I..."

But Max couldn't argue with his father, he'd never been able to. Somehow, everything his father said came out as the definitive final word.

"Yes Sir," said Max.

Max had felt small. His cheeks had started to redden.

"You are a disappointment my boy."

The words sliced through him, so easily said, so difficult to undo. His fingers had begun to shake.

"I expected more from you. But at this rate, you'll never amount to anything in this city." His father sighed. "Oh, how I'd hoped for more from you. But still, here we are. What's done is done. Now, you take responsibility for this, you hear? But remember, this is business my boy, that's all it is. That's all it ever is. You lost her, you get her back."

Max had nodded. "Yes Sir."

"I know what you're trying to do, but don't take it too personally. Just get her back."

His father's words had echoed in Max's mind all the way out to the ore mines.

"You are a disappointment my boy."

Well, I'll show him.

The aircraft vibrated. Far below, the wasteland stretched out in all directions, a vast, red, omnipresent emptiness. A world of dust and more dust.

Agrippa Panache, praetor of the city, his father.

One day, I'll control the ore mines, he thought. All that iron, all that steel. I'll take the coal mines too. I'll plate the city walls in graphene. I'll show him who's a disappointment. Business he says, but he makes it so personal. You're such a disappointment. I'd expected so much more of you. From each generation to the next, an endless cycle of inherent indignation. I'd like to rip his throat out. One day I'll take it all from him. I'll slip the knife in when he least expects it and tear open his jugular. We'll see what he has to say about that.

Max glanced out of the window as the ore mine came into view; a vast stepped terrace gouged into the red earth and hollowed out. Like an open wound, inflamed and infected, and at least two miles wide. The terraces crawled with moving bodies like insects, chained in lines, each oscillating back and forth with his or her own particular axe. The ore to build a thousand towers. Max's skin prickled. He hated to be beyond the city walls. This world beyond his own unnerved him. Involuntarily, he tapped his right foot against the metal floor panel.

On the landing pad, the hive of activity kicked up an ever-present dust cloud that coated everything and everyone in a fine red powder. Max held a handkerchief to his mouth. The muscular foreman had no such luxury. The burly man's torso was covered in tattoos; a fist, a skull, a dog with its teeth bared. Max had no desire to stray far from the aircraft. As the engines slowed, the sounds of thousands of pick axes emerged, metal on rock on metal on rock. There were a lot of people in the world with axes to grind.

"So you lost her," said Max, over the din.

"I didn' lose 'er. You lost 'er. I lost two good men. You lot owe me for those."

Outside the city, nothing could be done properly. Nothing was easy with these ill-educated outsiders.

"We paid you didn't we? You got the money."

"Ya pay us for the ore. Ya don't pay us to take care of ya children. That's your job. I did what ya said and I lost two good men. If you've a problem with any of that I suggest ya take it up with the big fella. We got a deal with you people but otherwise you lot don't mean squat to me out 'ere."

Dag it.

Deep in the wasteland, Max felt exposed. He listened to the idle hum of the aircraft engines; an island of civilisation in an age of barbarians. They were almost drowned out by the constant clang of pick axes. He hated it out here. He hated the stench of human labour and the metallic tasting dust that infused everything. Why did he need these people? But he did and he knew it, however useless they were. And the plan had seemed so simple. What better place to hide Starla from the all powerful mayor than down a mineshaft? The mayor would have been forced to negotiate power. He would have never found her here, and Starla was his obvious weakness.

"So where is she then?" asked Max.

"Last I heard, she was bein' picked up in Cooper. Lost two good men of mine there."

"Cooper?" The salt plains. But that was Corinth's territory? The big fella.

△△△

"Max."

On her knees, Starla leant over the edge of the dark hole that had opened up beneath Max.

They should never have run away from the guards.

From the darkness, a small voice cursed. "Dag it."

Starla's heart began to race. "Max, where are you?"

"Where do you think?"

In the darkness, Starla caught the glint of Max's eyes. "How deep is it?"

"I don't know."

"Well, can you climb back up?"

"I don't know. I think I've hurt my leg."

Starla tried to lean further over the lip of the hole. Her hand slipped on a loose rock and she drew back quickly. She looked up, the new wall looked a long way away now, as did the old one behind her.

Maybe there were guards already stationed on the wall? But what if it was fully automated? What if there were only robotic construction vehicles? And weapons.

Max and me aren't supposed to be here. I'm not supposed to be here.

"Max, what should I do?"

Far below, she could hear Max straining like a trapped animal. His eyes glinted again.

"Max, I'm going to find help."

"No, don't. My father would kill me."

"And you think mine won't?"

"Starla, don't go."

"I'll be back soon."

"You can't tell him, you can't."

"I'll be back, Max."

"Starla…"

Starla stood. She turned and began to trace her way back across the cleared land. She could hear Max crying, trapped down the hole.

"Starla come back."

Her heart beat deep in her chest. A few meters away, she collapsed on the ground. Who could she go to?

I could find a guard. I don't have to call my father or Max's. But word was sure to make it back. We'll be in so much trouble. But what else can I do?

For a moment she felt paralysed. She looked

back at the hole, then back towards the city. But what else can I do?

She picked herself back up and made her way across the broken ground. Max's calls disappeared beneath the hum of construction crews.

Later, the guards came and rescued Max, but after his time in the hole, his reptilian green eyes didn't pulse quite as brightly. And Starla guessed his father was probably very angry. He didn't run off again.

△△△

"How did you know I was on the outside?"

For a moment, Max was quiet. He took another step closer. "Well, once we'd checked your rooms and the zoo, where else would you be?"

Starla took a step backwards. "I don't trust you Max. This isn't right. You're playing games."

"No games, Starla. You know I don't play those games."

"Max, you were always playing a game. Even when you think you're not, you are. You can't help it."

"Dag it, Starla." His face was turning red. "For one second would you just do what you're supposed to do."

"And what's that Max?" She took another step backwards, towards the stairway leading off the platform. "Marry you? Hand you the keys to the city? Go into exile for you?"

Max took another step forward and the guards followed.

"Starla, you've gone crazy out here. And we don't have time for this. Now come on."

"I'm not crazy Max."

"All right, fine." He turned to the guards. "Get her."

Starla turned and fled down the stairs, back onto the walkway that ran along the top of the dam. She ran towards the riverbank. One of the guards fired and Max screamed.

"Fire at her and I'll fire at you." Then he called down; "Starla, it's time to stop this. There are bigger things than us Starla. And there's nowhere left to run, not this time."

Starla ran along the top of the dam and almost tripped over the lifeless body of Jirra. He lay twisted on his back and stared lifelessly upwards.

I'm sorry, she thought, I never meant for this to happen to you.

She stumbled onto the riverbank and ran up the metal pathway. The wound on her leg was screaming again. She hobbled up the rocky hill beyond, tripping on the loose rocks. She got to the top, lost her footing, and tumbled down the other side.

She came to rest at the bottom. Her heart galloped and her fingers shook. Her arm was bleeding but it didn't hurt, her ankle however did.

Max set this up, I just know it. This is some

kind of power struggle, some political game.

She hobbled to her feet and a stabbing pain shot up her leg. She looked down and the wound on her leg was bleeding again. She looked around for a place to hide and saw a small cave hidden among the rocks. She limped over to it and wedged herself down inside. There was a space just big enough for her to squeeze. Her arm was beginning to hurt too and dark red blood was dripping down her elbow, smearing the wall of the tiny cave. Tears came to her eyes but she stifled them down. She was too angry to cry. On the rocks above, she heard footsteps. Nearby, a few small rocks tumbled down the hillside. Starla started to shiver.

She remembered being cornered in the back of the van. She remembered the look of glee in the older man's eyes as he contemplated assaulting her. A cold feeling crept into her stomach. She shuddered and held her breath.

CHAPTER 31

Ari remained hidden under the panel. She heard Max order the guards after Starla. This was an ambush. Carefully, she crawled out from under the panel and peered over the windowsill. Starla was on the riverbank, hobbling up the rocks. The guards pursued her. Max stood at the edge of the landing platform, his hands on the rusty railing and his back to Ari. He was calling after Starla.

"...and there's nowhere left to run, not this time."

Ari slipped the blade from its sheath on her ankle. She moved slowly and carefully, keeping her body low, around the panel and through the doorway onto the landing platform.

The platform creaked gently, a warm breeze moving across its flat metal surface. The stationary aircraft ticked as its panels cooled.

Ari held her breath and moved quietly forward. Her heart thumped against her breastbone.

She could almost reach out and touch Max. Underfoot, a metal panel creaked.

Max spun around, his eyebrows raised, his mouth twisted, and then he lunged for Ari, pushing her over and knocking the blade from her hand. Max landed on top of Ari and pinned her arms down.

"Well, what do we have here? The girl from the outside."

Underneath Max, Ari wriggled. His breath smelt strangely sweet.

"Now come on sweetheart," said Max. "I'm flattered, but you're really not my type."

Ari tried to reach for her blade. Her finger touched the edge of the handle, then it pushed it away.

Max gripped one hand around her shaven scalp, the other across her jaw. He pressed the back of her skull against the hard metal floor.

"I mean, is this haircut really what passes for attractive in Cooper?"

Max's fingernails pressed into her cheeks. Ari wriggled and, with her freed hands, tried to reach around his broad shoulders.

"I think I'll just break your neck now, I've no other use for a girl like you. But I want you to know, so that perhaps you might derive some pleasure from it, that I am going to enjoy this."

Ari thrust her knee into Max's groin and his angry grimace collapsed. Ari kicked him again and he removed his hands and rolled sideways off her.

Ari rolled the other way. She grabbed hold of her blade and sprang to her feet. Still on his knees, Max reached inside his long jacket and pulled out a handgun. Ari kicked it away and it slid over the edge of the platform. Then Ari kicked Max hard in the face. When he lifted his head again, red blood seeped from his nose. Ari tried to kick him again but he rolled away. He held one hand out as if to surrender. With the other, he covered his bleeding nose. He looked pathetic and for a moment Ari held back. Seemingly taking his chance, he rose and fled back to the aircraft.

Quickly, Ari descended the stairs to the walkway along the top of the dam and ran towards the riverbank.

Then the guns on the aircraft opened fire.

Bullets popped along the walkway near Ari's feet. Ari leapt sideways and fell hard onto the metal platform below. Here, she was sheltered from the guns.

I should have finished him, she thought. I should't have hesitated, not for a moment.

Where she'd fallen, her right side felt tender. She got to her feet and started limping along the lower platform towards the riverbank. Then, close by, another bullet clanged. She pulled herself against the metal wall. Something damp trickled down her right arm. She felt around the wound and when she looked at her hand it was red.

Dag it, she thought. A dull ache began to form in the upper part of her arm.

Cautiously, she peered upwards, and spied Max on the upper walkway, pacing back and forth, swinging a pistol in one hand while, with a handkerchief, he intermittently dabbed his red nose.

"You're dead now," he said.

Ari didn't think he could see her.

She crept along the wall, keeping well against it. Max fired the pistol again and the bullet ricocheted a few feet from her. Then, via a stairway close to the middle of the dam, she saw Max climb down onto the lower platform. He fired towards her and Ari hunkered down behind a steel column. When she peered around, he fired again.

Ari felt like her heart was in her mouth.

She could hear Max's footsteps getting closer. Ahead, the rocky embankment formed a steep wall. To get onto the riverbank, she'd have to climb back onto the upper platform. Then she looked at the bulb of water expanding away from her before going through the dam.

Close by, Koora's body lay face down, a dark pool forming around it. Ari looked at the fuse wire running just above her head. She looked at Koora then back at the fuse wire.

Koora, I really hope you knew what you were doing. This better work.

She pulled her fire-starter and flint from her pocket. She placed the fire-starter against the fuse wire. She took a deep breath and then struck the fire-starter twice with her flint. The second time, the spark caught and the fuse wire burst into hissing orange sparkles. Ari hunkered down close to the floor, ready to jump. It was the only way.

CHAPTER 32

Starla hid in the tiny cave and tried not to make a sound. The guard made their way down the slope, swinging their gun left to right. A crisp blue uniform and tall black boots. The guard's face was opaque, hidden by the black helmet's full-face visor.

Starla prayed; please don't let them see me, please don't let them see me. Turn back now or go on past but please don't see me.

Starla tried to push herself deeper into the tiny space. Her heart raced. The muscles in her calves tightened and her skin began to crawl.

Please, please don't see me.

△△△

The fuse wire hissed and fizzled until it reached the first sack of gunpowder.

This is it. Do or die.

Ari leapt.

From beneath the waves, she heard a thunderous boom and a ripple surged through the water.

$$\triangle\triangle\triangle$$

Starla's heart leapt. The ground shuddered and loose rocks tumbled down the hill. Briefly, Starla feared the cave would collapse.

The guard paused and turned towards the direction of the explosion.

$$\triangle\triangle\triangle$$

The explosion triggered a chain reaction right along the dam. One after another, the sacks of gunpowder exploded, ripping holes right through the metal structure. By the time the explosions reached the middle of the dam, the weight of the water pressing against it was splitting it clean in two. The centre collapsed inwards and aircraft and platform went tumbling into the water. A wall of water heaved through the dam breach.

$$\triangle\triangle\triangle$$

The ground continued to shudder and more loose

rocks tumbled down the hill.

What is happening, thought Starla? It feels like an earthquake.

The guard began scrambling back up the hill towards the dam.

Gingerly, Starla worked her way out of the cave, each movement hurting a different part of her body. She peered up the hill. The sunlight caught the guard's helmet before it disappeared over the brow. Cautiously, and following the path the guard had taken, she too began to climb the hill.

△△△

Ari surfaced, gasping, and scrabbled desperately at the warm water. Ahead, she saw the dam open up like a giant metal jaw. The air was torn apart by the painful sound of twisting metal, while the heavy current dragged her towards the open mouth of the dam.

Tension rose in her gut; a hot, heavy feeling surging towards her fingertips. She clawed with open hands at the water.

Come on, she told herself. Starla could do this. Starla could jump in the water and swim. I can do this too.

But the hard water dragged her forwards, while she flailed, trying to keep her head above the waves.

Ahead, a huge section of what had just recently been the walkway hung down into the water.

Ari tried to manoeuvre herself toward it but before she could manage this she was already on it. Her body thumped against its hard surface. She tired to grab at it; its metal edges scraped at her fingertips and she kept on moving.

The torn edges of the dam rose up around her.

She caught hold of a rusty handrail.

She gripped it hard, then the powerful water engulfed her and she was underwater. Submerged, her ears bunged. The warm water clawed at her body, trying to drag her on. Her heart thumped faster as she felt her fingers being prised from the handrail.

She screamed into the water and dragged herself forward, increasing her grip. She tugged at the handrail, getting both hands on it.

Come on she told herself, you have do this.

The rail twisted in her hands but she kept on pulling, one hand after another, summoning her every ounce of strength. Her head broke the surface. She turned her face from the current and it dragged heavily on her neck. Her muscles seared and the top of her right arm stung to the bone. She got her feet on the platform and dragged herself up, out of the water.

The platform shuddered and creaked, at any moment ready to give way and join the rest of the dam down river. Ari cried out and pulled herself up the platform. One hand in front of the other, slipping on the wet metal, close to the top the walkway was almost vertical. Legs dangling in the air, she dragged herself the last few feet to the top, her right arm screaming, and rolled over the edge onto the solid ground where she lay gasping. Staring up at the pale blue sky, her whole body shuddered and her hands felt like they'd been stripped of their skin.

Then a bloody hand reached over the edge of the embankment and grabbed her.

CHAPTER 33

The bloody arm tugged at Ari's waist She was dragged right to the edge of the riverbank. She reached into the sheath on her ankle and pulled out her blade. The fingers clawed at her. Over the edge, she saw Max's twisted grimace. Half his face was seared away and his eyes bulged. She tried to twist from his grip. His fingers clung to her vest. She raised the blade.

"Don't move." The first guard was moving quickly down the hill, his gun raised at Ari. The second guard was moving from the other direction along the riverbank, his gun also raised.

Ari held the blade above Max's throat. He gurgled, his eyes meeting hers.

Starla appeared at the top of the hill. "Stop," she cried.

The second guard swung his gun and levelled it with Starla.

Starla raised her hands.

Ari gasped. "Kill me an' he dies too." She lowered the blade to Max's larynx.

Starla stumbled down the hill, her arms still raised. "I'll do what you say, just don't shoot her."

Briefly, they all looked at each other; Ari with the blade over Max's throat, the first guard with his gun on Ari, the second guard with his gun on Starla. A warm breeze flowed along the riverbank. The water, surging and splashing down in the river, was beginning to calm. Somewhere, a bird squawked.

Then, as if from the sky, a spear burst through the first guard's chest.

The guard dropped his gun and collapsed to his knees, impaled midway along the length of the spear, which now protruded through his sternum, ending at a bloody point. Ari, Max and the second guard all turned to look at him. The guard's body shook, his arms outstretched, his helmet gazing upwards. Briefly, he looked as if he might be praying to the eternal baking sun, the merciless true ruler of the wasteland. And then he fell forwards and was still. The end of the spear had propped him upright. Slowly, his body began to slide down the shaft.

Ari turned back to Max and raised her eyebrows. She drove the blade into his neck. He rasped, as if trying to say something, and he released his hand from her vest. Sliding off her blade, he dropped into the rolling water below.

Gasping, Ari rolled over and looked up at the

second guard.

The guard took a step backwards and swept his gun between Ari and Starla.

Ari looked about herself and then carefully got to her feet. Her blade was covered in blood and her hands were shaking. Her whole body ached. She looked at the guard. "Figure it's up to you now."

The guard stood motionless. Then he lowered his gun and dropped it on the ground. Slowly, he undid his helmet and lifted it over his head. Underneath was a boy with sandy blonde hair and tired, frightened eyes that were notably brown. He dropped the helmet and raised his arms.

"I only wanted to save Miss Corinth."

CHAPTER 34

Starla dropped her arms and stumbled the rest of the way down. From the other side of the hill appeared the tanned, gangly figure of Doug, his eyeglasses glinting in the sunlight. The guard watched Doug warily as the Angu man came to the edge of the riverbank and inspected the destroyed dam.

Ari stepped forward and took the gun from the guard's feet.

The guard was shaking. "Please," he said. "I'm just here to rescue the mayor's daughter."

"Well," said Ari, "Ya gotta strange way a' goin' about it."

"Please." He looked at Starla. "I am only loyal to your father."

Doug pulled the long spear from the other guard's chest.

Starla looked at the guard. There was something familiar about him. "My father sent you?"

"No, I am assigned to the Panache family. But when I saw what Max was doing I knew I had to try to help you. Please..." He looked back at Ari. "You have my gun."

Ari looked at Starla then back at the guard. "What's ya name?"

"I'm Guardsman Janus."

Ari indicated to Starla. "Ya know 'im?"

Starla studied the guard carefully. "You were at the party."

The guard nodded.

"You tried to warn me."

"I had to try."

"I think he's okay," said Starla. "Can you get us back to the city?"

The guard looked over the riverbank. Downstream, in the middle of the river, was the wreckage of the aircraft. One wing and a hunk of black fuselage protruded from the water. "Well, I can't get you there in that."

"But we can walk?" said Ari.

The guard nodded. "Yes."

"She comes too," said Starla, indicating to Ari.

The guard gulped nervously and nodded.

Ari turned to Doug. "What about you? Where ya gonna go?"

Doug scrunched his eyebrows together and looked towards the sky. His eyes bulged beneath his eyeglasses. "I'll go back to the village."

Starla turned to him. "I'm sorry about Jirra

and Koora."

Doug sighed. "They'll be right. Jirra and Koora will return to the earth. No one really dies, it's all a cycle. An' we destroyed the dam. The river will flow the way it should now, just as Maka wants it. Maka has a plan, ya know." He looked at Starla. "A plan for you I think. Back in Alice."

"I'm sorry anyway," said Starla. And she really was. Seeing Jirra and Koora gunned down had been entirely senseless. These people had helped her, in ways no one had done before.

Ari turned back to the guard and raised the gun.

"All right then, Guardsman Janus. Let's get goin'. Maybe we'll make the city by sundown."

CHAPTER 35

At dusk, within the city's high walls, lights like landlocked stars had started to appear among the jagged skyscrapers. From their rocky outcrop, Starla, Ari and Janus watched the multi-coloured lights blinking into existence across this sealed forest of steel and glass. It was as if, for too long, the city had been unable to grow in any other direction but upwards. It was a city seemingly desperate to escape the barren world with which it was tethered.

Between them and the city, the plain had dried to powdery talc, void of all moisture, its only feature the shallow channel of the barren riverbed.

When Starla had first caught glimpse of the city, a series of shimmering towers, glinting far off in the open sun, her heart had leapt. By this point, she was sure she was close to collapsing from exhaustion. A deep pain throbbed in her leg, and every bone in her body ached. She was thin and hungry, her face stung, and her throat hurt every time she swallowed. Yet now she sat, staring from the outside, at the city that, until only a short while ago, she'd never left. She'd made the journey back, and it was all down to Ari. This girl was her saviour, and now, just maybe, she could be hers.

"There she is," said Ari. "Alice." She carefully tightened the bandage around the top of her right arm.

"I can't believe it," said Starla. She tried the telephone in her arm. Beneath the skin, the lights flickered then disappeared. The gash on her arm stung, though the wound had sealed. She must have damaged the telephone in the fall. But they didn't need it now. They were so close, they could walk right up to the wall and knock on the gates.

"Ya better believe it," said Ari. "Come on, let's keep movin'."

As night fell, and the city grew brighter and the plain grew darker, the road south from the city was marked out in a series of wavering orange lights. Closer, Starla could just make out the silhouettes of camel trains and people.

Ari paused. She indicated to the gun in her hands. "This thing ready to go?"

"Yes," replied Janus.

"Who are those people?" whispered Starla.

"What I was afraid 'a I reckon. They guard the road. Most work for the big fella. They'll be lookin' for us."

"Can they see us?" asked Starla.

"How do I know?" said Ari.

"What do we do?"

"I dunno."

"Look," said Janus. "Before we start shooting at each other, why don't I go ahead to the gate? They're not looking for me."

Ari looked at Starla.

Starla shrugged. "Why not?"

"Why not, 'cause then that's the last we 'ear of 'im."

"Ari, what do we have to lose?"

Ari sighed. "Fine."

The guard nodded then sprinted off into the darkness.

"This is a trap," said Ari.

"We have to trust him."

"Well I don'. I don' 'ave to trust no one."

They moved closer to the gates, keeping to the darkness. Yellow lights shone down on two giant, metal gates, standing slightly open. Animals were being unloaded and ragged people were hauling sacks into great piles.

For a closed city, thought Starla, there was plenty of activity at its gates.

Then, beneath the yellow lights, Janus appeared. He approached the opening between the gates, then went inside.

"Well, e's in," said Ari. "Ain't no reason for 'im comin' back."

"We'll give him a chance."

"Don' see why. We're gonna 'ave to get passed these guys. Just gonna 'ave to chance it."

"No, wait."

Ari sighed again.

"Look," said Starla. "We go now, what's to stop these guys from shooting you and taking me? We're so close but the city's not running things on this side of the wall."

"Fine. But if 'e's not back soon..."

They stood silently in the darkness.

Come on, thought Starla. So near and yet so far.

Starla imagined the despair so many from the outside must have felt, to be so close, and the gates even open, yet entry to the city remained impossible. The opaque walls, dark on this side, stretched upwards and outwards, an impenetrable barrier. Here, a person could wait for months, staring up at the wall, hoping beyond hope that something might change, that someone might let them inside. Finally, when all hope was lost, they'd turn back to the lawless road, or the swamp and the desert. This was what Ari must have felt, after her parent's died and she found her way back to the city. This is where hope was born, and where hope died its death. So near and yet so far, to a city with so much yet so little to share.

Starla thought again of the words from Velle Stella. A world without borders, without walls. And she thought of the words of her father. But Ari didn't want to destroy the city, she only wanted a better life. A life she'd been denied. And with the simple fluke of birth, a life denied so many. And for some perceived security, what price too did the city dwellers also pay?

"You've been here before," said Starla.

"Yeah," said Ari. "Two months I was 'ere. Waitin' an' waitin', gettin' hungry, gettin' thirsty. Only thing ya can do 'ere is unload the camels, or worse. No further though."

"I'm sorry," said Starla.

"Ain't no ones fault."

Starla wasn't sure that was true. However remotely, perhaps a lot of people were responsible for those two months, and all the years in the wasteland that came with them. The skeleton by the tracks, the old man in the desert, the wild, desperate look in the milky-eyed man's single iris. And Ari, starving in a cave, dreaming of home.

Janus reappeared at the gates and Starla released a long sigh. Several other guards followed. When Janus reached them, he looked shaken. One of the guards was pointing a gun at him.

Another guard asked, "Miss Starla Corinth?"

Janus managed to smile at Starla and Ari. He'd come through for them.

Starla stepped forward. "Yes."

The guard produced an electronic screen. The screen flickered and the face of Starla's father appeared. Still the silver hair, the bright red tuxedo, but in other ways he was not quite the man she remembered. He looked tired and maybe a little older. Grey stubble covered his chin. His eyes were red and, having lost their permanent squint, were wider than she'd ever seen them. He smiled warmly, but when he spoke there was the slightest crack in his voice.

"My dear, thank goodness. I was so afraid I would not see you again. There has been a terrible betrayal. Please, let these guards bring you inside the city at once."

Starla hesitated. It was actually good to see her father again, and he looked so tired, he must have been worried. There seemed to be new lines around his eyes, or ones she'd not noticed before. In a way, it was as if she was seeing her father for the first time; she wasn't sure she'd ever seen him look so human. But, Starla wasn't going to break her promise.

"This is Ari." With her hand, she gestured towards Ari. "She saved my life and guided me here. I promised her a home in the city."

Starla's father drew back and grimaced. His eyes narrowed. "My dear, I'm sure she did, but is her home really in our city?"

Starla looked at Ari, then back at the screen. "Why wouldn't her home be in the city? She helped me. Has she not earned her right to return?"

"She left?"

"As a child."

Her father paused. For a moment, his red eyes seemed to glaze, then they hardened.

"My dear... to return once you have abandoned our city. That alone would set a dangerous precedence. Others would follow. You must understand, I must uphold the law, and our way of life..."

"Our way of life! What does that even mean? I'm your daughter. If she's not coming in, I'm not coming in."

Her father's eyes widened and his voice faltered. "But Starla my dear, what are you saying?"

"Please Starla," said Janus.

"I'm not and you know me, I won't. That is my line Father." Starla was back in her rooms, laying down the law. She was her father's daughter. She was better than her father even. She would not back down from what she now knew to be right. "You know father, maybe we should open up the gates. Maybe we should let them all in. Maybe our way of life is wrong. Maybe I don't believe anymore." And in that moment, Starla truly meant what she was saying. She'd been on both sides of the wall and on neither did she like what she saw. Besides, how could her father place the city before her? How could he argue, after all that she had been through in order to return to him? He hardly deserved her efforts. She could have stayed in the wasteland and abandoned the city and the glass tower that had, for so long, been her prison. "Father, if she's not allowed in then you shall lose me forever."

Her father paused. His face deflated and the

weariness returning to his eyes. "Very well," he said. "As you wish my dear, this girl may join us."

Starla's heart leapt. She turned to Ari. But Ari had taken a step backwards.

"We can go home," said Starla. "We both can."

Ari looked to Starla, then to the screen where Starla's father eyed her warily.

"I dunno," she said. "Ya know I don' think the city's for me."

Starla's face fell. "But Ari. What do you mean?"

"I see it now. See, my place was always out 'ere, even when I was in the city. So you go ahead. I got other places to be."

"Like where?"

Ari shrugged. "I dunno. Maybe I'll go back to the village. I wouldn' fit in in Alice ya know. So this is as far as I go."

Starla shook her head, tears forming beneath her eyelids. "You have to come with me."

"Na, you'll be right. Ya don' need me now anyway. Though I reckon you'd 'a made it here anyhow." Ari grinned. "Ya tougher 'an ya look sister."

"Please," said Starla. "That's not true. I do need you."

"Listen to your friend Starla," said her father through the screen.

"And you can shut up," cried Starla to her father.

Ari stepped forward and took Starla's hand. "Ya know, I ain't never met anyone like you. You're amazin'. But ya belong here. I don'. This ain't my world, I see that now." Ari reached into her pocket, drew something out, and pressed it into Starla's palm. Then she reached up and wiped a salty tear from Starla's face. "But who knows? Maybe one day it will be. Until then, you keep these."

Ari leant forwards and gently kissed Starla on the cheek.

"Well sister, be seein' ya round maybe." Ari winked at Starla and her pale eyes sparkled. Then she turned and walked away.

Starla collapsed on her knees and watched until Ari had disappeared completely into the darkness. She tightened her fingers around the two lashes. She tried to speak but nothing came. A lump grew in her throat and she was more alone then than she'd ever felt before.

CHAPTER 36

The city Starla returned to felt cold and sterile, and its people seemed shallow, preoccupied with trifles that no longer seemed important. And with the Panache family gone, Starla found herself alone. Liviana was gone, but so was everyone with whom they were ever connected. And there was no more talk of marriage. If the power succession still bothered her father, Starla saw no hint of it. There was even a rumour that, when the time came, Starla would rule the city alone. But for now at least, her father was more powerful than ever.

At society gatherings, where once those attending kept their respectful distance, they now actively avoided Starla. She'd been on the outside, a stigma that was difficult to escape. But her family name was also a little more dangerous, and Starla didn't know which one of these factors repelled people more. What she hadn't expected was to feel so acutely the resulting loneliness. She'd found a new status; an exile within her own city, and in her isolation she never did discover the exact details of her botched abduction, or what the Panache family had hoped to gain from it. And if her father knew the details, he didn't share them with her.

Once Starla had confronted her father, specifically to know the whereabouts of Liviana. Starla had always thought she'd no time for Liviana, but now she missed her. At parties, she wondered what terrible hair colour Liviana might have chosen. At the zoo, she missed her bored companion. Had Liviana been a part of Max's plot? She had deliberately spilled the champagne, but had she deliberately spilled it for that purpose? Her father had told her not to worry about such things, that the Panache family were being dealt with. And Starla suspected her father had spied an opportunity to cement his power and be rid of the Panache family all together. But was Liviana now in exile somewhere in the wasteland?

Janus became Starla's personal guard. For his efforts he was promoted. Sometimes Starla caught him watching her, and she felt slightly safer for it.

As time passed, Starla would frequently find herself gazing out into the wasteland surrounding the city and wondering what became of Ari. Ari had left behind an emptiness in Starla's heart that she couldn't easily fill. Now in memory, Ari seemed nothing more than a ghost, one of the many that haunted the world beyond the walls.

At night, Starla would wake from some nightmare or other and would wonder where she was. She would expect the silence of the desert, huddled under a salt sack, shivering in the cold, and instead was met with the hum of the air conditioner and the traffic moving far below and the twinkling lights of the city refracted through her window blinds onto the dark walls of her bedroom. And on nights like these, she would go to the big windows and look out over the luminous cityscape, and she would let her eyes wander, from the chasms of steel and glass and blinking lights, to the inky blackness beyond.

Occasionally she would look up, to the star that never moved. She no longer thought of it as her own, or Velle Stella, now it was the Maker star. She would think of Jirra, and what he'd said about the wall. And, she would remember the words of the voice from the sky and the dream of a world without borders, for this was what the wall undoubtedly was. A physical barrier that separated one group of people from another. The more she thought on it, the more pointless the wall seemed. It was too arbitrary. Now the outsiders had faces, and ones she couldn't hate. And the face she thought of most was Ari's.

One girl who'd almost achieved the impossible and broken through the wall. Where she was now, Starla could only guess. Like the old man, she had crumbled back into the red dust. Now, the world beyond the wall was once more a mystery, but one Starla couldn't easily forget. And, nor could she forget the girl with the shaven head.

The salt digging girl.

The orphan girl.

The girl called Ari.

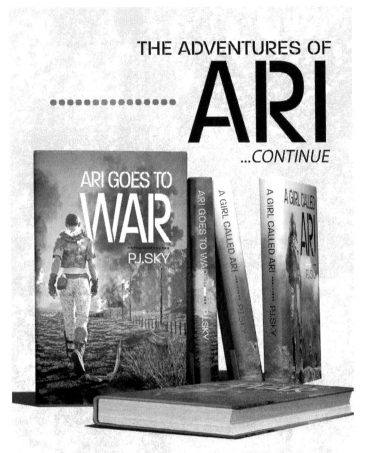

SPECIAL THANKS

No writer can work entirely alone, therefore I would like to give special thanks (in no particular order) to: Katherine Moore, Guy Russell, Maureen O'Brien, Karen Guyler, Colin Hurst, Keren Stiles, Alan Stiles, Autumn Sky, all the members of Writing Group, all the members of Now Write, all the members of Monkey Kettle, and all the friends and family who've supported me, proof read, and generally been there when I needed you.

You know who you all are. Thank you.

Printed in Great Britain
by Amazon

59685408R00166